To Orv
Tl

Eric Price

# UNVEILING
# THE WIZARDS' SHROUD
## SAGA OF THE WIZARDS: VOLUME ONE

Eric Price

MuseItUp Publishing
Canada

Unveiling the Wizards' Shroud © 2015 by Eric Price

All rights reserved. No part of this book may be reproduced or transmitted in any form or by any means, electronic or mechanical, including photocopying, recording, or by any information storage and retrieval system, without permission in writing from the publisher.
The characters and events portrayed in this book are fictitious. Any similarity to real persons, living or dead, or events, is coincidental and not intended by the author.

MuseItUp Publishing
14878 James, Pierrefonds, Quebec, Canada, H9H 1P5

Cover Art © 2013 by Charlotte Volnek
Layout and Book Production by Lea Schizas
Print ISBN: 978-1-77127-717-4
eBook ISBN: 978-1-77127-448-7

*For Allison, who made me do it...*
*without you, this would only exist as a file on my computer.*

# Acknowledgements

I'd like to thank everyone who read my early draft: Allison, Annette, Eric H., Lynn, Mike, Nate, Scott, Shannon, and my parents. The final product barely resembles what you read, but many of your comments made their way into this version. Thank you, Erin, for some last minute pointers. And my editors Nicole and Katie—you made it shine!

# CHAPTER ONE

# The Festival

The late afternoon sun glared in the young warrior's eyes. Squinting, he could only see his opponent's outline. His ever tightening leg muscles cried for a reprieve with each step, yet he continued to circle, waiting for the perfect opportunity to strike. After a long day of sword dueling with little downtime between rounds, Owen's whole body screamed for a rest. But he wanted nothing more in the world, at this precise moment, than to win the championship bout.

His opponent must also be tired. They had each fought four previous matches, and every contestant entered in the tournament presented a worthy challenge. Edward, Shield of the King—the commander of the King's Sentry, the strongest army in all of Wittatun—received continual praise for his skill with a blade. Owen, having already defeated two Sentrymen earlier in the day, hoped to beat one more. But to overcome the King's Shield would require more skill than besting a Sentryman of lesser rank.

The fighters continued to circle one another. Sunlight gleamed off Edward's brilliant metal chest plate and helm. Now facing the westering sun, the Shield of the King squinted. The younger fighter saw his opportunity and sprung. He feigned a slash toward the commander's shield hand. When Edward raised his shield and braced for impact, Owen redoubled his assault.

He spun and sliced his blade at his opponent's neck. The loud clang of steel on steel resonated throughout the courtyard as Edward raised his sword to parry. The vibration transmitted up Owen's arm, but he finished his compound attack by kicking the Sentryman in the chest

1

2 | ERIC PRICE

plate. The judge blew a whistle to signify the landing of the first blow in the best-of-three veney.

The experienced warrior wasted no time mounting his counterattack by gaining the measure and reestablishing just distance. He made several quick jabs at Owen's head and chest, which the defender parried away with ease and countered with a testing jab. Edward sidestepped, moved back in line, and raised his sword to the en garde position. The younger fighter noticed Edward's shield drop ever so slightly. The tiny gap in defense may provide the opening needed to finish him.

Owen lunged. He recognized the move as a mistake, but his forward motion could not be stopped. The tip of Edward's sword slid between the hinge where the chest plate met the shoulder guard and dug into muscle. Sharp pain shot through his left shoulder, and he barely heard the judge blow the whistle through the anguish. Edward had lowered his shield as an invitation for a strike. When the younger fighter took the offering, the elder's stop-thrust found the only weak point of the armor.

Owen, large for his age, still stood six inches shorter than the Shield, whose muscular forearms resembled Owen's thighs. The chainmail armor on his forearm, form fitting on most soldiers, clung tight to Edward. His muscles rippled as he pushed the sword tip a little deeper into the meat. A stream of blood trickled down the blade and dripped to the ground.

Edward sneered. Red drops splattered the trampled grass. "I wish we fought to first-blood. I hope the king doesn't put me to death for injuring his son."

"You don't need to worry about my father," Owen said between breaths, "you're fighting me. Besides, I've been hurt worse training with the defense master."

"Time to finish it."

Owen should have stepped out to remove the blade from his shoulder, but that would have made him vulnerable to an attack as his opponent still held tight to the sword handle. Instead he cast aside his shield, seized the other blade with his gauntlet, and spun away from his opponent. Thereby, he pulled the hilt free, but also made the point dig deeper into his own shoulder.

Owen removed the weapon to a bittersweet mixture of agony and ecstasy. He flipped it, snatched the hilt, and spun back to face his opponent. He unleashed a barrage of slashes and thrusts with both hands. Weaponless, Edward could only try to hold off the attacks with his shield. Owen swept his leg to trip his opponent. The instant Edward jumped, Owen sprang up, driving his uninjured shoulder into the commander's chest. Edward crashed to the ground, and the whistle blew twice to signify the end of the match.

Owen put the point of one sword to Edward's neck as a symbolic coup de grâce to the mock battle. The spectators, compacted into the grandstands, erupted with approval.

"It's good this isn't a battle to the death," Owen teased, "or my father would have to replace the commander of his army. Of course, he may anyway, since you can't even defeat someone half your age and size."

Edward gave Owen an appraising glance. "You have fought well. The defense master speaks highly of your skill with a blade. Seems I was wrong to doubt his touting. Let's take a look at your wound."

Owen's face flushed hot over the mistake. How could he fall for an obvious ruse?

He removed his helm, and his dark, wavy hair, matted with sweat, fell into his eyes. He blinked hard to stop the sting. The cool, early evening breeze refreshed his tired body. He helped Edward regain his footing, and together they removed Owen's shoulder guard. Blood covered most of his upper arm and chest, but the flow had slowed to a trickle. The healer rushed to the men with a bucket of water and some bandage wrappings. With the congealing blood washed away, the cut, about the length of Owen's thumb, looked clean and straight.

"Don't move your arm, Master Owen," the healer said. "When you move, the cut gapes open and tears. You'll need to change this wrapping daily. I don't think it needs stitches, but if it is still bleeding tomorrow, find me or another healer to get it stitched. It will be sore for several days."

The healer finished the bandaging. Edward made his goodbyes and returned to his duties with the King's Sentry. As the crowd dispersed, the two people Owen most wanted to see approached from the east. King Kendrick walked tall, with his curly hair and waist length cape blowing behind him in the breeze. Following him, Owen's best friend, Yara, a commoner about his age, kept pace at a subservient distance. She always kept her brown hair tied back in a ponytail that fell about halfway down her back. With her steps, it bounced from one shoulder blade to the other. Her slender, emerald green dress hung to her ankles, and she raised the skirt slightly to keep the hem off the ground.

Yara demonstrated unnecessary subservience. King Kendrick was not the kind of leader to mind her walking next to him as an equal. She had lived most of her life at Innes Castle until her family moved to Innes Village three years ago. But Owen knew she believed in the importance of certain societal customs, and showing the utmost respect to the king of the Central Domain topped the list.

"Congratulations, Owen!" King Kendrick said. "What a tournament. You defeated a street fighter, a sorcerer apprentice, and three members of the King's Sentry, including the King's Shield."

"Thank you." Owen's chest puffed up with pride. "I don't mean to sound arrogant, but I would have been disappointed had I lost. I work very hard at my battle techniques. The defense master told me I'm the most dedicated student he has ever taught, and he taught everyone on the King's Sentry, including Edward."

"He also taught me," his father added. "I'm proud of you, son. And I'm especially thrilled since I held the tournament in honor of your fifteenth birthday. However, I must bid you ado. Mansfield has returned from his voyage to the west, and he is presenting his findings to the council soon."

Explorers from the neighboring Western Domain had discovered a new continent far across the Ocean. The king had sent his best scout to investigate the native people: to learn about their culture, to find out if they had technology to traverse the ocean, and most importantly, to discover if they were friends, or enemies.

He addressed Yara. "Will you and your family be able to attend the feast this evening?"

"No," Yara said. "We are receiving this year's supplies of metal today. Father said I could either have the day or evening off, but not both. I chose the day because I wanted to make sure Owen didn't do anything extreme in the tournament." She stole a glance at his bandaged shoulder. "Besides, I'm just not that comfortable at fancy banquets at the castle, nor are Father and Mother. They do send their gratitude for the invitation."

"Good evening, then." King Kendrick looked at his son. "Don't be late for the feast. You know I have something very special planned."

"Yes, Father." Owen frowned when Kendrick turned away, suspecting the feast would bring an unwanted announcement.

When Kendrick was out of earshot, Yara asked, "What is that scowl about?"

"The same thing I've been telling you for the past year. I know what his surprise is. He's going to name me heir to the throne."

"Well, you are his only son. Who else is he going to name as his heir?"

"I'm not his legitimate son," Owen explained yet again. Kendrick had never married his mother, as the Law of the Land prevented royalty from marrying commoners. When the king started seeing Queen Andrea from the Northern Domain, part of him hoped they would get married, so his father could name her son, Weylin, his heir. "I'd much rather fight on the King's Sentry than rule the land from a throne."

"Sometimes you have to accept your place in life," Yara said. "I'd like nothing more than to join the King's Sentry myself, but they have that silly old law about no women joining the Sentry. That's why you *need* to be king. You can overturn some of these laws."

Owen snorted. "So much for accepting your place in life."

Yara smiled.

Owen finally gave in and returned the grin. "I guess you're right. I could be the daughter of a weaponsmith and only inherit a hot pile of coal. Instead I'm the bastard son of a king and get to inherit the throne."

Yara's grin grew even wider, and she punched him in his uninjured arm. "Exactly! I have to run. Father will be wondering what's taking so long. And I think I can hear a pile of coal calling me."

He watched as she raced across the courtyard toward the village. Her ponytail earned its name by looking like the tail of a trotting pony while she ran, and her dress flared out behind her. While growing up together, they had learned from the same tutors, and she knew him better than anyone.

He walked back to the castle to change into his formalwear in preparation for the dreaded feast. He spent as much time as possible with Yara and wished she could attend the feast. Having her there wouldn't change the king's announcement, but it would help to lessen the sting of being named heir. Though right now, he was glad for a moment of solitude to collect his thoughts.

An uncommon amount of people jammed the corridors of Innes Castle, and many stopped Owen to congratulate him on his championship victory and his birthday. That prevented him the time he needed for thinking, but it helped keep his mind from the surprise his father had planned. According to the Law of the Land, an illegitimate child could be claimed as an heir anytime on or after the child's fifteenth birthday.

Rounding the corner into a hall that opened to the courtyard of the Keep, he saw someone he tried to avoid at all costs: the king's magician, Cedric. The man's thick, black beard with streaks of gray stretched almost to his waist. His black robe had white specks throughout. Is that the color of the material, or filth? He had the hood of his robe lowered to his shoulders, and a nest of unkempt, black and gray hair encircled his head like a wreath. Owen couldn't even hide in the throng as the once crowded corridor seemed empty all of a sudden. He pretended to study the stained-glass windows lining the hall. Each frame depicted a famous battle from the glorious history of the Central Domain.

"Good birthday, Master Owen," Cedric said. "And congratulations on your victory. I watched the final bout. I hope that wound isn't too deep." Cedric reached out and touched Owen's shoulder.

Owen spun and threw the magician up against a post. He paid no heed to his injury, throbbing since the sword pierced him, now hurting no more than a slight ache.

"Keep your filthy hands off me, sorcerer! What are you even doing in this corridor?"

"I came looking for you. I thought I should heal your wound."

Owen gave the magician another shove before releasing his hold on him. "I don't need any of *your* kind of healing. You've done enough for my family. I don't even know why Father permits you around. At the very least, he should have put you out on the street like the dog you are."

Not waiting for a response, he hurried down the hall, across the courtyard, and up the stairs to his room.

*Filthy mage. I can't believe he would even offer me his help.*

He rotated his arm and realized, with surprise, the pain had quieted to a dull throb. He threw his shoulder guards on a shelf, ripped off his chest plate, and peeled off the bandages. The open wound, still bleeding when he left the courtyard, looked almost healed.

"That monster healed me without even asking my permission!" he shouted at his reflection in the mirror. He would inform the king, but his father would tell him he was acting ridiculous. He wished Yara was coming to dinner. She would understand. She hated magic and magic users as much as he did. Owen couldn't decide what made him angrier: the mistake he had made, which had caused the injury, or that fool Cedric healing him with magic.

By the time he recovered his temper, all but the peak of the sun had fallen below the horizon, creating shadows all over his room. He lit a few candles and polished his armor and sword before putting them away, but it took him longer than normal. He couldn't stay focused on the task at hand. His mind jumped from the surprise, which he knew meant the king claiming his birthright, to his foolishness during battle, to Cedric and his unwanted magic. The last thought made his mind go deeper down a path he refused to tread, not when he had a formal dinner engagement to attend. He gave up and shelved the armor. It had an acceptable shine, but it fell well short of the meticulous effort he usually exerted on such tasks.

He changed into his formalwear and made his way to the dining hall, guests already crowded the length of the expansive table. Joyous, noisy chatter seemed to make the walls and ceiling swell. He eased around clusters of people toward his seat at the right hand of the king's empty chair. From a distance, he realized the disgusting magician had chosen the seat next to his. *At least he combed his hair.* But he forgot about that little detail when he realized someone unexpected sat to the left of the king's chair. Her long, black hair flowed midway down her back, and her elegant, icy blue gown seemed to reflect every light in the room.

"Queen Andrea, I had no idea you were coming!" Owen exclaimed when he reached his seat. He kissed her hand in a warm greeting. Could Queen Andrea be the surprise? Had he been fretting for no reason all along? He noticed the young man sitting across the table from her. "And Weylin! How are you?"

Weylin stared absently at the table, making no indication he heard his name.

"Weylin," Queen Andrea said, "Owen spoke to you. Please answer him."

He raised his head and made half an effort to smile. "Hi, Owen." Then he returned his gaze to the table.

"I'm sorry," the queen said. "We just arrived, and he hasn't had a chance to adjust. He doesn't travel well, and the Northern Straits were particularly rough. More than a day has passed since our ship made landfall on the northern shore of the Central Domain, but as you can see, he just isn't himself."

"That's all right," Owen said.

"I didn't know we were coming, for sure, until a few days ago, so I asked your father to keep it secret." She lowered her voice so it barely rose over the din of the dining room. "We had a bit of an uprising of sinister magic users in the Northern Domain. I think they may have even had ties to the wizards, but I don't know for sure."

Owen trusted Queen Andrea as an ally against magic, as her husband, King Leopold, died at the hands of wizards. He wondered whether Cedric overheard their discussion in the noisy hall, and if he would consider it a much-needed warning, but he looked to be engaged in conversation with the same sorcerer's apprentice Owen had defeated in battle earlier, so he probably didn't hear them at all.

Fighting the young sorcerer proved very interesting. The tournament rules forbade the use of magic, but the apprentice demonstrated remarkable agility and showed great skill wielding a staff. Owen suspected he had cheated and used magic to increase the speed of his attacks, given how close the match had ended up.

"Well, I'm glad you're here," Owen said. "You too, Weylin. I hope you feel better soon."

Weylin lifted his head and nodded.

Musicians crowded into the hall through the great doors, lined the walls, and prepared to play as an accompaniment to the meal. Two trumpeters stationed themselves on either side of the doors.

Kitchen attendants scurried around the table, making last minute preparations, filling drinks, and taking any special requests for food. One attendant placed a large loaf of bread in front of King Kendrick's chair, blocking Owen's view of Queen Andrea. She slid the loaf out of the way.

"Congratulations on your birthday," she said. "And I hear you won the tournament."

"Thank you. I fought well." He thought of his wounded shoulder and threw a distasteful glance at Cedric. "But not as well as I could have."

"Your father tells me he has a huge surprise to announce. Do you think—"

Before she could finish, the two trumpeters on either side of the dining hall's great doors sounded their horns to signify the king's arrival. All attendants arose. The doors swung open, and King Kendrick, dressed in a light green suit of clothes, entered. On his chest, the embroidered dark-green dragon, the king's family crest, seemed to project into the room. Four stewards followed behind the king, keeping his long cape from dragging on the ground.

The brightest star of the night shone through a window behind the king as he entered, despite the brightness of the room. It looked like the eye of an unknown beast peering into the dining hall.

Standing at his chair, the king commanded everyone to take their seats. The ruckus subsided, and King Kendrick began reciting his speech.

"Ladies and gentlemen of Wittatun, I thank you all for coming. Most of you come from the Central Domain, but I know some of you have traveled from faraway lands. We even have a special guest in attendance from the Northern Domain. Please join me in welcoming Queen Andrea."

Everyone clapped and cheered as Andrea half rose and bowed her head.

"This is a special day. I'm a busy man, but I am not a fool. And I'm not deaf. I know there has been enough gossip about my surprise announcement by the hoarse voices of many members of the quilting guilds."

Everyone knew most of the older ladies from Innes Village met once a month for quilting guild, but no one knew if they actually quilted or just stirred up local gossip.

"Well, it's time I put the tongue wagging to a rest, at least for a while. I never married Beatrix. I'm sure you are all familiar with the Law of the Land, so I will not bore you with the details of why. But she was a wife to me in every way except legally. Her death three years ago created a void in my life that can never be completely filled."

Owen felt his face grow warm with a mixture of remorse and anger. He scooted away from Cedric as much as he could at the crammed table.

"It's time," the king continued, "I move on from the loss and expand my family to fill as much of the void as possible."

*He's going to claim my birthright, making me his son and rightful heir to the throne.* The inevitable moment he had dreaded since before his mother's death. But nothing he could do would change his father's mind. Hadn't he tried everything? He scooted his chair back from the table to better enable himself to stand when his father claimed his birthright, making him, Owen, his legal son and true heir to the throne of the Central Domain.

King Kendrick stretched out his left hand. "I have asked Queen Andrea to marry me, and she has accepted."

Owen's mouth hung open. *A surprise announcement indeed!*

# CHAPTER TWO

# The Fall of King Kendrick

The dining hall erupted with clapping and cheers over the king's announcement. Owen sat cemented to his chair. *What?* Had his ears deceived him? He could think of no better birthday gift than this. If his father married Queen Andrea, the king could name Weylin heir. Weylin would make a better king anyway. He had more interest in politics than fighting. If he occupied the throne, Owen would be free to pursue a career with the King's Sentry. What a great surprise!

When the cheering subsided, Kendrick continued, "This union will not only bring together two broken families, it will meld two of the most powerful lands in Wittatun. The combined forces of our armies would make our lands virtually impenetrable to attack from outside forces, and we would have a strong alliance should the Wizard Rebellion ever rise again."

At the mention of the wizards, the hall filled with nervous murmurs mixed with some applause. Numerous feasts have occurred at Innes Castle since the Wizard Rebellion attacked, yet King Kendrick has only mentioned the tragedy once: at the first banquet following the onslaught.

"But I have more than one surprise for you tonight. I also have the business of naming my heir, and now I have a choice to make between my son," he gestured toward Owen, "and my soon-to-be stepson." His hand moved in Weylin's direction.

Owen's stomach sank when King Kendrick reached for the bread Queen Andrea had pushed away. *Of course!* The bread had seemed particularly large when it came to the table, but he hadn't realized its purpose. Now he recognized the affirmation loaf. All legal contracts, according to the Law of the Land, could be bound, or unbound, by breaking an affirmation loaf and sharing it with seven or more witnesses. He glanced around at the attendants leaning on the edges of their seats for the proclamation. This packed dining hall certainly constituted seven or more witnesses.

*How could I overlook an affirmation loaf?*

For the first time, a prickle of excitement, not dread, tingled up his back for what might come next. His father *could* name Weylin as his heir. He, Owen, may have the opportunity to try out for the King's Sentry after all.

The king raised the loaf above his head. "With this loaf, I claim my true heir." He broke the bread and tore it in two halves. A dusting of crumbs fell and landed on Kendrick's face. He made a face like he may sneeze, his eyes grew blank, and he gazed absently at the room. "I'd like… I'm going… I…"

King Kendrick stumbled and fell face first into the table. Blood gushed from his nose and smeared the white tablecloth. He crashed to the ground, and the two halves of bread flew from his hands and rolled across the floor.

Owen rushed to him, but Cedric arrived at the king's limp body first. The sorcerer started mumbling incantations under his breath. His scarred and calloused hands hovered over the lifeless body. The magic cleaned the king's bloodied face. Cedric stopped speaking, stood, and examined the dining hall from one end to the other. Not appearing to find whom or what he sought, he returned his attention to the king. Owen wanted to tell the magician to stop, to leave his father alone, but the shock of the moment left him paralyzed to do anything but watch and hope his father wouldn't die.

When Owen regained some of his senses, he stuttered, "Ced-Ced-Cedric, what-what's wrong?"

Cedric glanced at him through locks of hair that hung in his face, gave a slight shake of his head, and focused on his work.

Owen waited. He still wanted to tell Cedric to stop using magic on his father, but even as much as he hated Cedric, deep down he knew the sorcerer would do nothing to harm the king. Owen slammed his fist into the tiled floor. Pain shot all the way to his elbow, but he didn't care. He wanted to do *something!*

At last, Cedric stood. Keeping his hands over the body, he raised them to waist level, said an incantation, and elevated his hands over his head. The lifeless body of King Kendrick rose and hovered chest high. Cedric motioned toward the door, and Kendrick hovered through it.

Cedric took a quick look over his shoulder. "Owen, follow me."

Cedric walked with his hands outstretched, and King Kendrick's body floated before him. Magic propelled the king, and they followed the body down one hall after another. When they reached the Keep, Owen sensed someone following. He turned to see an empty corridor and resumed the pursuit of Cedric and his father up the stairs.

At Kendrick's chamber, Cedric floated the body to the bed and directed it to land with the head resting on the pillows. When Owen entered, Cedric waved a hand at the door. It slammed shut. The magician leaned over the body, mumbling incantations. At times, sparks flew from his hands and encircled the king's body. Again Owen had the urge to tell him to stay away from his father, but his fear of the unknown outweighed his fear of magic.

Cedric rose from the body and sped to the door. "I have to leave to mix a potion. If it doesn't work, I don't know what to do. I've exhausted my magical knowledge. Don't let *anyone* enter this room while I'm away."

Owen didn't have a chance to respond before Cedric rushed from the room. He walked to his father's unconscious body which looked as much dead as asleep. What could have done this? Poison? Magic? Could someone have sent an assassin for the king?

He placed his hand on his father's neck to feel for a pulse. It took a while, but he found a weak beat. He lost himself in joy. His father still lived!

A cricket chirped in the corner, and an owl hooted in the distance. If he strained his ears, he could hear his father's slow, shallow breathing.

Yet what was Cedric doing? Making a potion? Now that Owen had regained his senses, he couldn't understand how he had let the magician do so much. Was it wise to stand aside while the magician poured some concoction down his father's throat?

*But Father trusts him, even these past three years. He must have his reasons for allowing the magician to stay at the castle.*

He jumped when a knock at the door startled him from his vigil. Like waking from a dream, he stumbled to the door and opened it. Queen Andrea almost knocked him over as she rushed to the king's side. She extended a hand toward his head. A spark of electricity shot from his temple to her hand, and she jerked it away and shook it. Cedric must have put a protective spell on the king.

"Will he be all right?" she asked.

Owen shook his head. "I don't know. Cedric didn't say. He went to make a potion."

The queen approached Owen and took his face in her hands. "You unfortunate boy. What a horrible thing to have happen on this most important birthday." She embraced him in a hug.

"I'm still trying to figure out *what* happened. He looked fine. He held the bread—"

The door crashed open, and Cedric burst into the room. "What is *she* doing in here? I told you not to let anyone enter this room!"

"I don't know," Owen said. "It's just Queen Andrea. I didn't think —"

"That's obvious," Cedric said. "It doesn't matter. I've used magic to protect him. No one can harm him now. Please prop his head."

Queen Andrea released Owen, and he raised his father's head. Cedric took a small vial from his robes. He removed the cork and poured the contents down King Kendrick's throat.

The three of them stood and watched the king's motionless body for what seemed like an eternity.

Cedric walked to a window, rested his hand on the sill, and lowered his head. His somber voice did nothing to alleviate Owen's anxiety. "If it were going to work, it would have by now. That is the most potent potion I know. A terribly powerful spell felled the king."

Owen realized the truth of what he had started to suspect. "Do you mean magic did this to him?"

Cedric came away from the window and stood next to the bed. "Yes. A magic unlike anything I've ever seen before. I'm going to have to seek an old acquaintance of mine. If anyone knows what's happened here, he would. And I'm going to need your help, Owen. It's likely to be a long journey. Fetch a sword, armor, and a light pack of necessities."

Owen's vision turned red, and the surrounding noises muted. The nerve of the magician. He sucked in a deep breath trying to calm himself, but he couldn't hold his temper at bay. "I'm not going *anywhere*, you crazy old wizard! And I'm certainly not going with you to search for some other crazy old wizard. In case you didn't notice, my father's life is in danger."

The term "wizard" had taken on a new meaning since the attack of the Wizard Rebellion. Magic users, those not supportive of the Rebellion, considered the term an extremely vulgar profanity. Most non-magical people knew this as well. Owen knew it, but he didn't care.

Cedric ignored the obscenity. "That's why you must come. The journey will be dangerous, and it will take my magic, as well as your sword, to reach our destination. I will protect your father with the best spells I know. You needn't worry about him."

"We've seen the effectiveness of your magic. If you need a sword, take a Sentryman."

Cedric turned his back on the other two and started arranging the bedclothes. "With the king's fall, the person responsible for this may try another attack. It will be very important for the Sentry to have all of their numbers here at the castle. You have proven today that you are just as good with a sword as any of them. And this way you can *actively* help save your father, instead of standing around waiting for someone else to do it."

This struck a nerve, and Owen relaxed. He always wanted to be in the front line. Here an opportunity presented itself, and he was making excuses to stay within the shelter of the castle. He smiled despite his misgivings.

Queen Andrea placed a hand on Owen's shoulder. "Cedric's right. I'm sure he can protect your father, and I can look after the castle while you're away. With the announcement of my engagement to the king, the Sentry will respect me as their ruler while the king is incapacitated. I will send a messenger to Deadlock Castle stating my intention to stay here longer than expected."

Owen considered her words. "Whoever did this may try to attack you as well."

"Don't worry about me. Weylin will stay here."

Owen liked Weylin and thought he'd make a good king, but he questioned his ability to defend anybody. But Cedric and Andrea were right; he had to go on the mission. His shoulders dropped with submission. "Where are we going?"

"You needn't worry about that now," Cedric said. "Get your belongings and meet me at the front gate. Let as few people as possible know you are leaving." He turned to the queen. "Queen Andrea, you will have to leave this room now. I'm going to put a protective seal on the door."

Cedric's incantation resonated down the hall as Owen returned to his room. The farther he walked from his father's chamber, the less the magician's argument for leaving made sense. *How can I leave my father at a time like this? Cedric insists he needs my help, but what worth does a sorcerer's word hold? Yet Queen Andrea also thinks I should go. She despises magic for her own reasons, so she wouldn't mislead me.*

He supposed he had to go no matter how much he wanted to stay by his father's side.

And would staying at the castle make him weak? A coward? Cedric's comment about actively helping his father instead of standing aside while someone else did the work sunk deep. He desired to join the King's Sentry instead of ruling from a throne so he wouldn't have to wait while others risked their lives for him. How could he not exert his fullest effort to save his father, even if it meant traveling to the farthest corner of Wittatun?

Once in his room, Owen fastened his dragon-mail armor over a tunic. He spent countless hours listening to his father, with a booming voice full of superiority, recount the story of his ancestor, Frederick, how he defeated the dragon, Kartal, skinned him, and fashioned the dragon-mail armor. The unfamiliar sting of tears burned his eyes as he wondered if he would ever hear his father tell the tale again. He hadn't cried since his mother died, and he wouldn't cry now.

He blinked hard and grabbed his two-handed Claymore sword, swung it in his empty room a few times, and then put it aside in favor of the lighter broadsword he had used during the tournament earlier in the day. How long ago the tournament seemed.

Owen considered taking his gauntlets and his buckler but decided attack by beast far outweighed the likelihood of attack by person. He left them behind in favor of light travel.

The castle corridors were completely void of people. Everyone probably still waited in the dining hall to hear word of the king. Owen couldn't concern himself with them now. Queen Andrea could govern in the king's absence, and she would inform the people soon enough. Cedric must have ordered her to wait to address the attendants until they had a chance to gain ground on people leaving the hall.

Owen wanted to return to his father's chamber one last time before leaving, but he pushed the urge aside to buy time. He hoped to beat Cedric to the front gate so he could make a quick trip into Innis Village to tell Yara what had happened. What did it matter that Cedric instructed him to tell no one?

The moon and the flickering glow from the torches along the castle wall provided the only light. Two Sentrymen stood guard at the gate. He thought he had a chance to sneak out when a shadow below one of the torches moved.

"Owen, over here," Cedric whispered. "I have informed Edward of the events that took place this evening. He's the only person, besides the queen, needing to know we've departed. We have to leave now to stay ahead of the visitors to the castle. Follow me. We'll climb the barracks and grapple down the wall to avoid the main gate."

Owen hurried to him. "Will you tell me where we are going now? I'd like to tell Yara we're leaving. And I had to leave my dying father to accompany you." He still struggled with the decision to stay by his father's side, or seek the cure.

"You mustn't tell anyone where we head. Evil has long ears. And your father *isn't* dying. He could live for several months without food or water as I have him now. But you need to understand the significance of what we face. I will tell you what I know as we walk. Some of it you may know, some of it you will not."

To avoid the Sentrymen at the gate, they climbed the stairs to the ramparts. Owen's foot caused a tiny corner of stone to crumble and fall to the ground. In the absolute stillness of the night, the sound must have reached the Sentrymen.

Owen and Cedric pulled back into the shadows and waited. The closer of the two guards turned his head and looked around. He walked toward the stairs, and Owen held his breath. The soldier searched at his feet and peered up into the darkness. He must have satisfied himself that nothing was askew because he returned to his post without further investigation.

They ascended the rest of the stairs, Owen paying particular attention to step lightly. At the top, Cedric produced a grappling hook from his robes. He fastened it to the brick and lowered the rope. He descended first, followed by Owen.

As they crept through the castle grounds, Cedric quietly continued his explanation, "We have to find an old acquaintance of mine. I studied magic under Argnam, one of the most powerful magicians ever. I began my magical training at the age of twenty and completed my Endeavor by the age of twenty-five."

Owen had heard of the Endeavor: a task, or series of tasks, put upon a magical apprentice by his or her mentor. By completing the Endeavor, the apprentice would become a fellow of the craft—a true magician.

"My journeys have taken me to the farthest reaches of this land, to parts of the planet you don't even know exist. I have seen things you probably wouldn't even believe. Now, it's important that you understand my seriousness when I say, 'I have never seen magic like this before.'"

They shuffled their feet descending the dew moistened slope of the hill on which Innes Castle had been erected. The trees of the forest grew larger as they approached, and Owen had no desire to tumble down the hill toward them like a rolling cannonball.

The terrain leveled so they could walk normally, but they still crept softly, keeping their footsteps quieter than the surrounding nocturnal insects.

They reached the ends of the grounds, and Owen's tense muscles relaxed upon entering the cover of the forest. He cast one last look toward Innes Castle and the village, wishing he could have seen either his father or Yara again.

Even this far from the castle, Cedric kept his voice low. "You must also realize that anyone at the castle could have done this. Therefore I instructed you not to permit anyone into the King's Chamber. I tried to discover the culprit at the Great Hall. Directly after the attack is when he would have been most vulnerable, but whoever did it kept his actions in check."

"It had to be the apprentice," Owen said. "No other sorcerers attended the dinner, besides you."

"I don't think so. Talented sorcerers can disguise themselves, and this magic far exceeds the capabilities of an apprentice."

Owen tried to think of someone else who looked or acted strange. So many people attended the celebration that he had never seen before. He gave up when a wolf howled, followed by several more and the patter of paws. They faded away into silence, indicating the wolves moved away from the two men. *Nothing to worry about. They want to avoid us as much as we them.*

Cedric finished his story. "During my Endeavor, I met a very powerful magician. A *master* of the craft, a special ranking only bestowed on a select few. His intelligence far exceeded mine, or even Argnam's. Master's have more advanced magic than fellows, and they typically specialize in a particular area or areas. This master specialized in nontraditional magic, along with many other areas of study. He will know what to do if anyone does."

No wielder of magic impressed Owen, regardless of his or her experience. "Where in Wittatun do we find this so called magical genius?"

"The last I knew he resided in the Land of Fire."

Owen halted in his tracks. Did the magician really just suggest they stroll into the perils and scorching heat of the accursed land? He shook his head in disgust. "Did you say the Land of Fire?"

Cedric stopped and looked back at Owen, a casual expression gracing his face. "Yes."

"So we have to cross Death Desert?"

"Indeed, we do."

Owen could feel rage bubbling at his temples. His vision lost focus, and his voice sounded more like the grunt of a wild boar than a human. "You know I can't get beyond the outer rim! If the heat doesn't kill me, the animals will!"

"You can, and will, get through Death Desert," Cedric's mustache twitched as he attempted to smile through his mass of facial hair. "But we'll have to use magic."

# CHAPTER THREE

# Wizards

The thick forest surrounding Innes Village blocked out any moonlight. An owl screeched in the distance, as if it were mocking the inevitable use of magic. A wolf howled again, much farther away than the last time.

"Listen here, wizard!" Owen snapped. "I will not be learning any magic."

Cedric walked on. "Of course not. That's why I had you bring your sword. Diversity—the key to many of life's challenges." Cedric turned his head, his brow furrowed and his eyes narrowed leaving slits as black as the surrounding woods. "But I'm *not* a wizard, and I would appreciate you not calling me one. I have denounced them and their ways. The Wizard Rebellion tainted the word for all those using magic for good purposes."

"Diversity may be key, but magic has caused me more pain and hardship than it will ever aid me."

*What good could come of magic?* Owen didn't like the idea of depending on magic to survive the desert, regardless of who cast the spells.

Cedric's voice called out from deeper within the woods, "The hour draws late, and I can scarcely see in this forest. If my memory holds true, a clearing lies just ahead. We can set camp and build a fire there."

When Owen caught up, Cedric had already started gathering firewood. Owen helped, happy to end the conversation about magic. The trees parted above the clearing, and the sky shown bright with stars and the waxing gibbous moon. The huge star that had shown through the window in the dining hall, much brighter than all other heavenly bodies save the moon, now twinkled just over the tall peaks of the western tree line.

They piled the wood, and Owen went in search of food. He returned with three frogs from a nearby stream, their backs speared by his blade. Another trip to the stream resulted in a full lambskin canteen. He came back to find the fire roaring.

Cedric spun the frogs on a skewer made from a small branch. He removed the meat from the fire and distributed portions. "I know you hold magic responsible for what happened to your mother. You've made no effort to hide your hatred of magicians. It's no secret you blame me. I can tell you what really happened the night your mother died, if you'll listen."

Owen almost swallowed the frog's leg bone from which he sucked the meat. "No! I'm not talking about that with you. If not for you, she would have never learned magic. If not for you, the Wizard Rebellion would have never shown up at Innes Castle. If not for *you*, my mother would still be alive!"

"The Wizard Rebellion would have attacked Innes Castle had I been there or not." Cedric pressed his palms against his eyes. He shook his head, and hair fell over his fingers. "Owen, there's so much you don't understand. Magic is neither good nor evil. Evil people using magic, and their intentions, are what instill magic with evil. If you won't let me tell you what happened when your mother died, at least let me explain the Wizard Rebellion. You need to know how they began."

Owen thought about Cedric's offer for a moment. Without knowing where they needed to go or how long it would take to get there, he guessed several days constituted a conservative estimate. He may as well let the crazy old man tell his story. The magician wouldn't likely let it rest until he did. He took the last piece of frog meat from the skewer and poked the fire with a long branch before adding it to the fire. Embers sparked and floated away in the zephyr, burning out one by one.

"All right," Owen said. "Tell me about the Wizard Rebellion."

Cedric leaned back on a tree stump and talked. Owen listened with rapt attention to the story of how the Wizard Rebellion really started.

* * * *

The pitch black of the starless night sky violently erupted with lightning. The humid air had felt electric all day with the pending storm on the horizon. Now, nature would release all of her fury in a matter of hours. Trees would fall, and lands would flood. A gust of wind blew in through the cracked cabin window, snuffing out the lantern for the third time.

Tired of relighting it, as well as struggling to keep his newly acquired fire magic under control—a singed wall and scorched cuff on his robe accompanied the first two relights—Cedric fell back on easier magic. He took up a staff with a small sphere at the end, and he made the sphere glow a brilliant white-blue twice as lustrous as the lantern.

The light gave a purple hue to the face of the man sitting at the table reading a letter. Shadows formed in his sunken cheeks. He was lean but not unhealthy. The trick of the light made him resemble a skeleton. He ran a hand through his short hair.

"Thank you, Cedric," Argnam said. "I think I'll soon retire for the evening. Follum says the Eastern Domain passed a law restricting magic users to practice only within the confines of their own homes. He says he will journey to their land to discuss the foolishness of the law."

Cedric moved around the table to better see the note over Argnam's shoulder. Over a year ago, he had suggested they try establishing communication with those fearful of magic, but his mentor hadn't thought they would listen. "Have you changed your mind about reaching out to non-magic users?"

"Nay, Follum believes fear spawns from ignorance, and he thinks people can learn to trust magic. I don't share that optimistic world view. I've used my magic to heal fatal wounds, just to have the recovered person spit in my face for using magic on him." Argnam finished reading the letter. "Follum is right about one thing, we have to do something to stop the persecution of wizards. I've thought about organizing a rebellion. Give me another night to think on it, and we can discuss some ideas I've developed."

That night, Cedric dreamed of a great battle. Older, and now a true magician, he fought for his life. Others fought in the battle as well; some of whom he knew well, others he didn't. Yet in the surreal world of the dream, he knew everyone. And he understood where his loyalties lay.

A blue flash of light hurled toward Cedric. He jumped aside just in time. The magic slammed into the interior castle wall, causing it to crumble. In mid-dive, he charged his staff with strange magic he didn't yet understand. He rolled to his feet and propelled his staff like a spear at the familiar wizard who stood before him. The spear landed home and pierced the center of his former mentor's chest. Argnam had time to look down at the staff embedded in his chest before the staff exploded, killing him.

The next day, Cedric told Argnam of the dream.

Argnam fixed Cedric with a gaze that seemed to penetrate his inner spirit. "You know some wizards are dreamers. They can see the future in their dreams, but you've never had a seeing dream before, have you?"

"No."

"Then I wouldn't worry about it. I've never heard of a dreamer gaining the power as late in life as you."

"I'm only twenty-four," Cedric said.

"Yes, but you're almost ten years older than the typical age. Only once have I heard of a seer gaining the gift as late in life as sixteen. It just doesn't happen."

"I started my training in magic later than most. Do you think that could affect the onset?"

Argnam placed his hands on Cedric's shoulders. "Listen, I'm not going to worry about it, and neither should you."

Cedric closed his eyes and shook his head. "I'll try, but the dream seemed so real."

Argnam released the young man and took a seat. He gestured for Cedric to sit as well. "I'm sure it's nothing. Now I'd like to tell you about my plan."

They discussed forming a band of wizards with the purpose of traveling the world, seeking more wizards to join their ranks and attempting to convince non-magical people not to fear those who could wield magic.

As he thought over the plan, Cedric scratched at the stubble of the beard he had decided to grow a week ago. It itched so much. He didn't know how long he'd be able to keep at it. "And how do you suppose this…what should we call it, this Wizard Rebellion, should convince those who fear magic to trust it? I know you don't believe in *talking* sense into them like Follum does."

"We could hold demonstrations, public displays of magic. We could hold mass healing ceremonies. Anything to show people what good can come from magic."

Cedric shook his head. "When people hear wizards are banning together, they will pass laws to make our congregations illegal."

Argnam stretched his hands behind his head. A smug arrogance washed over his face, making it look more rigid than normal. "I've thought of that. We'll have to organize the wizards in secret. Keep our presence as quiet as possible. When we emerge in numbers, they won't have time to make laws."

A vision of Cedric's dream flashed in his head. He blinked to shake off the memory. "Some people may become violent. Fear is a great motivator."

Argnam rose and walked to a window. "If anyone raises a hand against us, we can use our magic to defend ourselves. Of course, a non-magic user couldn't do much to defend against one wizard, let alone many. So we'd have to be careful. Use our defensive spells sparingly. If anyone were to get hurt, it would set our cause back a great deal."

Thus the Wizard Rebellion started. The next day, Cedric made the first recruit when Necrose came to see if they, too, had received the letter from Follum.

A year passed. Many wizards in the Western Domain and Southern Domain joined the Rebellion. Argnam wanted to gain an alliance in the Eastern Domain before moving into the Northern Domain, due to the Northern Domain's geographical isolation. He intended to leave the political juggernaut of the Central Domain for last.

"Cedric," Argnam said, "the time has come for your Endeavor."

Cedric's mouth fell agape, and he dropped the goblet of water he carried. He had hoped to take on his Endeavor soon, but the mentor always determined the time, place, and event.

"I have received another letter from Follum. Remember a year ago when he went to the Eastern Domain to convince them their laws had to change? Well, it appears they prosecuted him, and he has spent most of the last year in prison. Your Endeavor is to rescue him, and, of course, find new recruits for the Wizard Rebellion while you're in the east."

Cedric made haste from the swamplands of the south to Echion, the capital city of the Eastern Domain. Once there, he bypassed the barracks and headed for the rocky cliffs of the seashore. One of the wizards he met along the way, and successfully recruited for the Rebellion, informed him the prison stood on a plateau that hung over the ocean.

Looking at the fortress, Cedric thought escape was too easy for a wizard. The rocky cliff and the ocean would deter a normal person from breaking out and leave them incapable of breaking in. With magic, he scaled the rock wall and made his way to the top of the prison, only to find it completely unguarded.

Inside, he didn't know where to start looking, but he didn't have to wander long. He held out his hand, and a fireball ignited and floated just above his fingers. The illumination showed an elderly man on a bunk in the cell straight ahead. Follum. Cedric extinguished the fire and charged the end of his staff. The faint glow it gave off reminded him of a dream he had forgotten long ago. *What had the dream been about? Had he used his staff to kill someone?* He snapped back from his memory and used the staff to pass the energy to the bars of the cell. They each gave off the same glow. He stepped back, and the bars exploded.

Follum sprang from the bed much faster than seemed possible for a man of his age. "What do you think you're doing?"

"Rescuing you," Cedric said.

Follum didn't act old at all as his tongue tore into Cedric. "You can't be serious. I am a master wizard. You are an apprentice. Do you think me incapable of breaking out of here if I so desired."

Cedric stood confounded.

Follum approached him with anger in his eyes. "I've remained to show the people of this land that I respect them and their laws. I hoped in time they would come to understand that I intend them no harm. Did you even face any guards getting in here? I bet not. And they moved me to this cell earlier today. Someone set you up. Let's go. We have to leave *now*!"

Cedric stared dumbfounded as Follum walked away. How could he have fallen for such an obvious trick? He followed Follum, and the two men hurried down the cliff wall and back toward the village.

"We'll follow this path toward Echion and hide in the forest."

Cedric still pondered who could have set him up. "Argnam sent me to rescue you as my Endeavor. No one else knew the plan."

"Congratulations! You're one of the craft now. You saved me." Follum turned on Cedric. "You're also a fool. He must have sent word of your coming. Let's take this path and hide in the forest."

Cedric *felt* like a fool. He thought he needed to explain himself. "We formed a rebellion to fight the injustices wizards face. We want to show people that magic can help them. I had hoped you would join us after I rescued you."

"Peaceful demonstrations have been tried before. They never work. At some point, they get out of control. The peace turns to violence, and the original cause looks worse than it did before the demonstrations. No, I will not join you. Argnam should have known I would refuse. I think your whole Endeavor is a test of your loyalty to Argnam."

*Could Argnam have set me up to test my convictions?*

Just before they reached the canopy of trees, countless soldiers emerged from the forest.

Follum made no effort to take a defensive stance. "An hour of judgment has come. Decisions made now will determine not only our fate, but the fate of all magic users in the eyes of the people of the Eastern Domain. I am prepared to wait out my days in prison. Yet we have come this far, and I will aid you in escape if you so desire."

Cedric considered his options. He could stand down with Follum. But he'd have to spend time in prison. He didn't share all of Follum's beliefs. While a fight could set back what little progress had been made over the past few years. "As long as we don't kill any soldiers, I say we fight. I don't believe rotting in prison will convince anyone to trust magic."

Cedric waved his staff, and the front line of soldiers flew back, knocking over the next two rows. Follum joined in the attack, and the two wizards worked their way into the forest and out of the Eastern Domain.

* * * *

By the time Cedric finished, the large, bright star in the west had progressed east to light the night sky directly overhead. He claimed exhaustion and settled down to sleep.

Owen lay awake pondering the tale. The information confounded him. This fool just told him he started the Rebellion, yet the Rebellion from the story didn't seem at all like the one he remembered. *Cedric even gave the Rebellion its name. And helped recruit new members. I wonder how many of the members he recruited were involved with the bombardment of Innes Castle?*

To clear his thoughts, he reminisced about his mother while he watched shooting stars burn across the clear night sky. Before long, his eyes grew heavy. Sleep overtook him.

CHAPTER FOUR

# Magic and Sword

Owen awoke before Cedric. He returned to the stream to bathe and drink. The bright star now hovered just over the eastern horizon, still radiant through the brushstrokes of purple, orange, and red painted by the pending sunrise. His rested mind returned to Cedric's story.

*Cedric helped form the Wizard Rebellion, yet Father trusted him. Had he known? He must have.*

The information should have fueled Owen's anger toward the magician, but somehow, he trusted the old man more than he did the day before. He trusted him more than he had for the past three years, to be honest with himself. Seeing the magician try so hard to save his father must have established *some* of that certitude, but he thought the story played a role as well. Yet, Cedric hadn't told him everything. He had said the Wizard Rebellion would have attacked Innes Castle had he been there or not.

*Why?*

Nothing in the story even resembled the Wizard Rebellion as he remembered it.

While he returned to camp, a faint glimpse of golden sun peeked over the eastern horizon and caught Owen's eye through the dense green and brown forest. Once there, he found Cedric awake and in the process of packing away their belongings. "Good morning. I filled our canteen," Owen said

The older man nodded as he packed. "Great, we'll need all the water we can get. This is the only stream we'll pass before we get to Death

Desert. If we make good time today, we should be able to reach the desert by nightfall."

The sun rose, and they finished packing their gear. The temperature cooled in the thick, shadowed parts of the forest. But each clearing they passed burned hotter than the last. As they walked, Cedric finished his story about the early days of the Wizard Rebellion and how he had come into the graces of King Kendrick.

* * * *

Cedric and Follum fled for two days before they felt confident the soldiers from Echion had lost their trail.

Before parting, Follum took Cedric's hand in both of his. "I wish you well, Cedric. I don't agree with your tactics, but I think your intentions are noble."

"Where will you go from here?"

"The Land of Fire has always been my home. The sparse population of the Western Domain results in little persecution for magic. I can stay isolated until I see reason to work against people's ignorance. After word of our escape gets around, I think the Eastern Domain will be lost to our cause." Follum released his hand, started to walk away, paused, and turned back. "Be wary of Argnam, Cedric. I've known him a long time, and he has often been my most trusted confidant. But his ideas have grown more extreme, and I don't trust his role in your mission to rescue me."

Follum took three steps to the west and disappeared. Cedric had heard of wizards having the ability to teleport, but he thought strictly sinister wizards possessed the gift. He would ask Argnam about it, right after he found out why his Endeavor involved freeing a wizard perfectly capable of escaping on his own.

He walked all night and returned to Argnam's refuge near the swamp early the next morning, only to find the land crawling with magic users of all different skill levels. Two stood as guards at Argnam's hut. Hagen, an old friend of Cedric's, recognized him and admitted him.

Argnam rose to his feet and ushered Cedric in by an arm. "Welcome home. How did you fare at your Endeavor? I see you're alive, so you must have succeeded. Tell me all about it."

Cedric jerked his arm out of Argnam's grip. "I need *you* to tell me something first. Why was the entire Echion army waiting for my arrival?"

A look of puzzlement stretched across Argnam's face. "When? Before you reached Follum?"

"No, I didn't see even one guard before I rescued him. Earlier in the day, they moved him to a cell at the exact spot I broke into the prison, as if they expected me. Not until we tried to return to the forest did we meet the army.

"Follum thinks they knew of the escape attempt, and I think he's right. He also had some questions about why you would send a wizard apprentice to rescue a master. He says he could have broken out at anytime, but it wouldn't have helped his case in convincing the people of the east to trust magic."

Argnam thought with his fist to his forehead, massaging his furrowed brow with a knuckle, as if debating a ponderous idea. Argnam lowered his hand and smiled before grasping Cedric by the shoulders. "Follum does not understand my ways. He and I could have been great comrades, but he always opposed my tactics. And, to be fair, I also opposed his."

Argnam's grip tightened. The young wizard realized how powerless he would be to defend himself against an attack from his mentor.

"I *did* tell them you were coming," Argnam said.

Cedric jerked to break Argnam's grip, but the long, bony fingers held fast.

"I knew Follum could easily escape without help. I also knew you could just as easily break in and rescue him. I sent a letter to someone I trusted in the army. A young man I met several years ago who considered studying magic before deciding to join the army. I instructed him to send twenty soldiers to stop you. This way you would face more of a challenge to test your full understanding of magic. I'm not sure what happened. Someone with a higher rank must have intercepted my letter."

This did sound like something Argnam would do, but part of his mind screamed not to trust the man. Still, he had studied under this man for so many years. Surely he could be trusted. Cedric relaxed, and Argnam's grip released him.

Argnam motioned toward the door. "Come outside with me. Wizards from across Wittatun have gathered. Our numbers grow, and with it, our strength increases." He continued to explain as they walked. "Tomorrow, a small group of us will make our first demonstration in Tuulikki, a town less than a day's travel by foot from here. Necrose and two wizards from the Southern Domain have agreed to join me. I would like you to come as well."

Argnam led Cedric down the passageways in their makeshift wizards' village. "The Tuulikki city council has a meeting scheduled to vote on a law that requires all residents trained in magic, even just a casual training, to register their names and abilities at the city hall. This will lead to further discrimination and prejudice. Skilled huntsmen and trained combat fighters are not required to register, and they pose much more of a security threat than any magical novice."

Argnam shook his head and looked dismal. "Holda, a small town in the Central Domain, passed a similar law. The fear of magic grew, and now it is illegal to have a staff or any other magical talisman within city limits. I fear similar action in Tuulikki."

"Of course I'll go," Cedric said. "We have to do what we can to deter this way of thinking."

The five wizards set out before midday. Excitement passed between them like lightning as they discussed the importance of this first true mission of the Wizard Rebellion. They traveled through the night and reached Tuulikki before suppertime the next day.

The wizards marched into city hall and requested a meeting with the council members. An old man who identified himself as mayor said he would arrange it. He told them they must wait as all five council members worked for different departments within the city, and it would take time to call an impromptu meeting.

The wizards waited in the library, and Argnam told his group that the willingness of the mayor to gather the council members surprised him. He had expected more resistance as their apparel must have identified them as a band of wizards.

After a lot of time passed, Cedric became nervous that the council must be plotting an attempt to capture the wizards. He decided to voice his suspicion when the doors opened, and five men entered, without the mayor. They introduced themselves as the councilmen and escorted the wizards to a meeting room.

The council heard Argnam's complaints regarding their law, and an open debate ensued.

The council chairman stood. "Mr. Argnam, I assure you the intention of the council is not to single out magic users. We feel the safety of the town lies in understanding any special abilities any villagers may possess."

"A fighter with a blade can do more damage than most magic users," Argnam said. "In fact, many people who have learned to use magic have only learned to use it to *heal* themselves and others."

"The problem isn't so simple," the chairman said. "Most people carry blades. Swords can defend against swords, but they have little ability to defend against magic. A person has a right to come to city hall and see if his new neighbor practices magic."

A councilman to the left of the chairman stood to address the wizards. "Look at it this way. Let's say magic users list their abilities, and a wizard has the capability to heal wounds. Then someone in need could use the list to seek their assistance."

Argnam jumped to his feet and slammed his fist into the table, knocking over two water goblets. "That's preposterous! In the society you describe, wizards will be stripped of their privacy and used as town healers. That's assuming they aren't all persecuted and removed from the city as soon as the law passes!"

"Mr. Argnam," the chairman said, "please have a seat. You're becoming irate." He reached for the hilt of his sword.

Before his fingers touched it, Necrose sprang to her feet. She thrust out her hand, and a red streak hit the chairman in the center of his chest. He collapsed to the floor, dead. The rest of the council rose to their feet. Two of them fled the room, but the other two drew their swords.

"Stand down, wizards!" one said.

Argnam raised his hands. Similar red streaks originated at his fingertips and ended in each councilman's chests. They, too, fell dead.

"Argnam!" Cedric shouted. "What happened to peaceful demonstrations?"

Argnam inspected a fallen body. "Necrose did what she had to, and so did I. They had intentions of attacking us. I could see it in their eyes."

Spit flew from Cedric's mouth. "We could have stopped them from attacking without killing them! Now three people are dead, and the whole town will want *us* dead!"

"They had their minds set against us before this meeting started," Necrose said. "I could tell, and I think you knew it too. They confirmed their intentions when they made to draw their swords."

Cedric gestured toward the bodies and dropped his shoulders in defeat. "People are dead."

Argnam stood and headed for the door. "If we don't leave now, more than three will die today. We can argue about this later."

\* \* \* \*

Cedric sat on the trunk of a fallen tree. Owen took a seat next to him, delighted to rest. His feet ached from walking on the branches and brush on the forest floor. The dense woods thinned some time ago, and only sparse trees spotted the tall grassland. The cool shadows of the forest gave way to intense, late morning sunlight.

Cedric wiped sweat from his brow and squinted into the sun. "We escaped the village without anyone else dying, but a good many people waited for us outside of city hall."

"Did you break your ties with the Rebellion after that?"

"In my mind, yes. Argnam and I argued on our way back to the swamp. I defended my points, but I never let my true feelings show. Eventually I allowed him to think I saw the situation his way. I wanted to get back so I could tell some of the other magicians what had happened. Breaking the others' trust of Argnam seemed the only defense against the Wizard Rebellion repeating these events in a different community. Only by defeating Argnam could the Rebellion be disbanded altogether."

"But you didn't succeed. The Wizard Rebellion still survived to attack Innes Castle several years later." Owen paused to collect his thoughts. "My mother died in the attack. They came to find you. Argnam must have been furious with you for trying to disband the Rebellion, so he came to make you pay."

Cedric shook his head and stared at his boots. "No, I didn't succeed. I convinced many magicians to leave the Rebellion. I stopped thinking of *all* magic users as wizards, even before the rest of society adopted it as a hateful term for those in the Wizard Rebellion.

"Some would not leave Argnam, however. They could not believe he would kill innocent men. They thought I must have deliberately added, or removed, details from the story to use it as propaganda against their leader and the Rebellion."

Cedric stood and stretched. His back cracked. He turned left and right. Each direction added another loud crunch of bone on bone. The older man extended a hand to help the younger to his feet. "And you, Owen, have lived these past three years with a misconception about what happened the day your mother died. It happened almost ten years to the day after the slaying at Tuulikki. Argnam brought the full force of the Wizard Rebellion to Innes Castle; although, the number of wizards he brought paled in comparison to the force he had several years earlier. The Rebellion came to Innes Castle, where I had lived for the past seven years, but they did not come to kill me."

Owen cast Cedric a doubtful glance but took the hand still dangling in front of him and stood. "How do you know they didn't come to kill you? It sounds like you gave them good reason."

"They had no idea I resided at Innes Castle. They already thought me dead."

## CHAPTER FIVE

# Life Vow

Owen and Cedric ended their rest and resumed their course. The trees became sparse, and the grass changed from a thick, uniform, healthy green to a sporadic patch of brown, dead grass and weeds. Strange birds unlike any near Innes Village called out as the travelers passed.

Cedric kicked a clump of dead weeds. They tumbled until they hit a rock. A dust devil spun away from Cedric's boot in the breeze. "We're approaching the outskirts of Death Desert."

"I've been here before. I came here with Father to hunt fire hounds." He checked the sun to see how much time they had before it set. They didn't need to worry until dusk, but they had to prepare themselves for an eventual attack. As a group of only two, the hounds would think them easy prey.

"I think it's time you know how I came to live at Innes Castle. Argnam discovered my tactics of convincing others to leave the Rebellion. I had planned my eventual escape, as I knew he would soon discover my ruse. I left maps and notes concerning the Western Domain in my quarters. I had corresponded with Follum about the possibility of joining him in the Land of Fire. I hid these letters but made sure anyone searching my lodgings would find them.

"Most of the people I convinced to abscond from the Rebellion stayed and worked with me to persuade others to leave. Had they all fled, Argnam would have grown wise to me sooner. Also, I expected I would need their protection, and I did."

Owen couldn't believe he felt empathy for a magician, but the challenges of working behind the back of someone as powerful as Argnam, and the bravery it must have required, filled him with admiration.

"Necrose came to me, feigning a desire to secede from the Rebellion. She said she couldn't do it without me. She and I had grown close enough I could tell something was wrong. I assumed they suspected my actions, but they sent her to get proof. I fled before they had a chance to trap me but too late to escape unscathed."

Cedric's smacked his lips, cleared his throat, and took a long draw from his canteen. "Five Wizards approached, and I quickly ignited a fireball and sent it toward them. My comrades heard the disturbance and rushed to my aid. By this point, I had more allies at the Rebellion camp than Argnam did. We fought his wizards off and even killed a few out of necessity. I injured Argnam but only enough to slow him. We fled. Hoping they would search my room and discover the information about the west, I headed east. There I hid for three years."

The ground grew rockier as they ventured farther west. An animal let out a series of barks followed by a howl.

Owen snapped his head in the direction of the sound. "That may have been a fire hound."

Cedric gazed toward a second howl. "We'll have to keep our eyes open. The beasts are only one of the obstacles in the desert. This isn't far from the location where your father found me, all but dead."

Owen looked at the ground as if he expected to see his father's footprints. "What happened?"

"After hiding for three years and monitoring the Rebellion's much slower progress, I learned of Argnam's new base of operations. I decided I could sneak attack him and put an end to the Rebellion... I was so young, and such a fool."

\* \* \* \*

The cool night air blew in Cedric's face. His new beard, now reaching the neck of his cloak, ruffled in the breeze. He hoped the sound of rustling leaves and tree branches would help mask his own sounds as he sneaked behind Argnam's cabin.

With his staff, he drew the outline of a door on the back wall. He stepped away, and the line started glowing faint chartreuse. Within the outline, the wall almost vaporized to dust. It piled on the ground as quiet as a phantom. The chirping crickets didn't even break from their merry song.

Creeping through the makeshift doorway, he saw the figures of a man and a woman lying in bed. The moonlight cast enough of a glow for him to recognize the man as Argnam. The woman's long blonde hair obscured her face.

As he approached the side of the bed, he raised the dagger he brought for the assassination. He took a deep breath preparing to plunge it into Argnam's chest.

The woman's leg flashed out of the covers, striking him in the chest and knocking the wind out of him. She sprang from the bed. Her feet met his face in a rapid succession of kicks, topping the skill of a master fighter.

Gasping for breath and unable to stand, Cedric fell to his hands and knees and looked up at the approaching woman. The moon silhouetted her female form. Light reflected on her face, and he recognized Necrose before she raised her leg over her head and slammed the heel of her foot into his face. Total darkness enveloped him.

Long bursts of searing hot pain mixed with burning cold eventually awoke Cedric. The blaring sun distorted his vision and sent bolts of pain through his head. Each time his heart pounded, his vision filled with the sight of a woman's heel coming toward his face, but he recognized the hallucination and shook it away. He blinked a few times before he managed to hold his eyes open. Raising his head, he felt something hard dig into his neck, a metal collar. His limbs were bound with thick chains.

Argnam sat before him. He held a staff—Cedric's—and touched Cedric's leg. It felt like lava flowed toward his groin and foot. He screamed. Argnam removed the staff, and the pain subsided. He brought the staff to the other leg. Submersion in the icy Northern Straits could not bring a freezing pain like this. He let out another scream. Argnam lifted the staff, and the pain abated.

Argnam rose and walked in a circle around Cedric. "I'm glad you revived. Necrose really put a wallop on your head. Did you know she had such amazing hand-to-hand combat skills? Or should I say foot-to-head combat?" He cackled at his own joke.

He brought the staff to Cedric's shoulder, and the feeling of molten brimstone poured down his arm. Cedric shrieked.

Argnam pulled the staff away. "Enough fun. I *do* enjoy my torture, but I have a more indirect form of punishment planned for you. I don't get the immediate satisfaction this gives me, but knowing how much worse it will be for you will have to suffice."

Cedric mounted all of his magical energy to break the shackles binding him. He felt his face contort from the effort, but the chains didn't even move.

Argnam watched and smiled. "Do you feel that metal ring on your neck? That's a cursed collar. Quite an amazing talisman. Necrose created it as her Endeavor several years ago. I've just been waiting for an opportunity to use it. You see, Cedric, the wearer of this collar cannot use magic."

Argnam waved his hand at the shackles, and they dissolved into the ground. "Better? You won't need those as long as you wear the collar. I just like to use them for their aesthetic appeal. I wanted you to feel like I held you only with chains. More importantly, I wanted you to feel like you had a chance of escape. I wanted to *crush* that feeling of hope! How dare you try to destroy what I, what *we*, worked so hard to build! The Wizard Rebellion could have taken wizards from a minor class of citizen, feared and loathed in some places, and made us into the ruling class of the land."

The wizard kicked Cedric in the ribs. He gasped for breath and rolled over just in time to see Argnam point the staff at him. Again darkness embraced him.

The intense heat made sleeping uncomfortable. Why did he sleep, anyway, with work to do? Getting away from Argnam needed to be his top priority. The sun beat down and fried his exposed skin like meat on a skewer. The hard, dry ground under him radiated more heat. He opened his eyes and squinted to shut out the blazing sun. Loose dust blew from the boots of a dark figure stepping toward him, and he clenched his eyes against it. The breath exploded from Cedric as a foot smashed into his ribs.

"Oh good, you're awake," Argnam said. "I had hoped you wouldn't sleep too much longer. I really don't like this heat."

"Where…" The words caught in Cedric's dry throat as he gasped for air. He swallowed and choked on dust. When he finished coughing, he tried again. "Where are we?"

"You mean you don't know?" Even in his weakened state, Cedric could hear the sarcasm pouring into Argnam's words. "You must think you're so smart. All the time I spent looking for you in the Western Domain. I thought for sure you had come here after I raided your hut. But you fooled me. I can admit it.

"So I thought bringing you here to die seemed appropriate. Here in Death Desert, with no magical ability, I'd guess you could survive a day or two, if an emmoth doesn't kill you first. We passed a small herd on the way in, so you probably don't want to head south from here."

Argnam let out a short chuckle. "They gave me quite a scare. I teleported us right next to them. I had to levitate you here. I didn't have the energy to teleport again, and I couldn't carry you, so very slowly we crept past them. I thought one had decided to give chase, but it turned away."

Cedric struggled to pull himself to a sitting position. His ribs stabbed his insides with every breath and movement. He assumed they were broken. His head spun, and he took a short pause to make sure he wouldn't vomit. "Tell me something I have to know before I die. When you sent me on my Endeavor, did you intend for the solders at Echion to kill Follum and me?"

Argnam smiled. "No." He tilted his head back and let out a full bellied laugh. "Not really. I didn't care if they killed Follum. I've always known he would never join the Rebellion. But I never wanted you to get killed." He laughed some more. "In fact, I wanted just the opposite. I hoped you would kill the guards." Argnam rested on a boulder. He wiped sweat from his brow and looked off to the distance. "I always hoped you would succeed me as the leader of the Wizard Rebellion when my years ended. But you didn't see wizards as superior to those who can't use magic. I wanted to break that mentality. There's more to you. For some reason, you hold back on your magical ability. I can sense it within you. You put as much effort into keeping your magic in check as you put into creating the magic. I thought if you would slip, just once, and unleash your full force, you may be able to understand our superiority."

The wizard rose to his feet and headed south. "I wanted you to unleash your power to escape, but you managed to spare the guards. You returned to me, and I spared you. I decided if you remained loyal to me, another opportunity would arise to help you break your restraint. It did in Tuulikki, but again you held back. To make matters worse, you betrayed me. For that alone, I cannot permit you to live."

Argnam teleported without as much as a glance back. Cedric sat alone in Death Desert. He stood, blackness obscuring his vision, and he thought he would faint. Steadying himself on a boulder until his sight returned. He recognized a rock formation far to the west, and any hope he had of surviving sank. The Vestibule to the Underworld—a name that could never truly express the eerie feeling that came from looking at the formation—marked the exact center of Death Desert. What else would he have expected from Argnam? He determined his own location to be about half a day's walk east of the Vestibule, so he headed for the eastern edge of death desert with no supplies and no magic, but with just enough hope to get his feet moving.

\* \* \* \*

Sweat ran down Owen's face, soaking the neckline of his tunic. His hair felt long and matted.

Cedric, with his longer hair and beard, didn't seem to be affected by the heat. "I don't know how far I walked. I became delirious. First came hallucinations. I had seen mirages before, but the hallucinations appeared so real. I saw beautiful cities, waterfalls, even snow. I expended so much energy running to one of the cities I can't believe I didn't die. My mouth felt full of sand and tasted like tree bark. My skin had started to boil. My vision blurred, and the sun scorched my eyes. The delirium set in, and I became overjoyed and excited, as if something good were happening to me."

"Did you make it all the way to the edge of the desert?" Owen asked.

"Not quite. Your father found me unconscious. He had been hunting emmoths. He had wounded one and chased it farther into Death Desert than he wanted. That's when he found me. He took me to Allentown, a small town on the edge of the desert, just south of here."

"Yes, I'm familiar with Allentown." He longed to be in a town and out of the heat and couldn't imagine the suffering Cedric had endured.

"They cared for me. When I recovered some, I had them remove the cursed collar from my neck. Until that point they had left it on, thinking it some form of jewelry. It took three people working the mechanism in the back to release it. Once gone, I could feel magic surge back into my soul. I used my own magic to return myself to full health. I thanked the Allentonians and went to Innes Castle. There I pledged a Life Vow to the line of King Kendrick. As he saved my life, I would serve him until my death, either of old age, or until I gave my life for his."

Cedric rummaged in the pocket of his robe, removed a black metal band, and handed it to Owen. "I'd like you to have the cursed collar, Owen. I've kept it these years to remind me to never underestimate my enemies. But I give it to you as a token of friendship. It's equally important to never underestimate our friends."

*Did this foolish old magician really think of me as a friend?* But deep inside, the deepest corner where Owen hid all his secrets, he began to think of Cedric as a friend too.

Owen examined the detail of the engravings on the metal. The symbols looked mystic. He had never seen them before, nor did he know their meaning.

A faint crunch of gravel snapped Owen to attention. He shoved the collar in his knapsack and drew his blade. "Something's following us."

As if in response, a chorus of fire hounds gave their characteristic bark, followed by a long howl. It sounded like a dozen or more. Some of the howls were probably echoes off the nearby rocks because fire hounds rarely traveled in packs so large.

From the corner of his eye, Owen saw a flash of red fur. Without thinking, he slashed his blade, and one of the fire hound's legs flopped to the ground. The hound slammed into the ground and rolled to its feet. It retreated with his three remaining legs.

Two flashes of blue light emitted from Cedric's direction, and two hounds lay dead at the older man's feet. Another chorus sounded, seemingly no fewer in number than before.

A hound appeared from behind a bush and leaped at Cedric. Its claws ripped a patch of skin off his left cheek and knocked his staff to the ground. Another hound grabbed the staff and ran with it. Owen had never heard of fire hounds showing such intelligence. He started to chase after it, but it dropped dead. A stick appeared to protrude from its head.

Owen stood in amazement when another fire hound leaped from the bush straight toward his face. It crashed to the ground, dead, with a stick growing from its head as well. Now he could see the flight feathers of an arrow on the stick.

He turned to see if Cedric had a bow, but the magician stood empty handed, looking at the ridge of a large rock. Owen followed his gaze to see a young woman standing there with an arrow nocked to her bow. She let it fly, nocked another, and released it.

"Are you guys going to stand there and watch, or are you going to help me?" Yara shouted.

# CHAPTER SIX

# Stargazing

With Cedric's staff recovered, Owen wielding his blade, and Yara serving as a sniper, the fire hounds stood no chance. When only two remained, they halted their attack and fled deeper into the desert. Thirteen hounds lay dead. Yara slung her bow over her shoulder and climbed down from the boulder.

Owen found their packs, only to discover them soaked with water. The canteens had all been bitten and clawed, causing them to rupture. He threw the broken canteens to the ground and kicked them. "Just great. Here we are on the edge of Death Desert, and we don't have any water."

"I have my canteen," Yara said, "but it won't last the three of us long."

Cedric took the two canteens with the smallest tears and mended them with magic. "They're not as good as new, but they will meet our needs. Mending living creatures is a lot easier than mending objects. We can use some of these fire hound hides to make water-skins. They won't hold water as well as a canteen, but it will be better than dying of thirst."

Owen gestured at the desolate desert all around them. "Where are we going to get water?"

Cedric handed him the canteens. He held the head of his staff over an opening. The end glowed white before changing to a radiant blue unlike anything Owen had seen outside Azur Glacier in the Northern Domain. A misty vapor rose from the staff, and the end gleamed with moisture. A drop of water fell into the container. Another drop followed, and soon a steady stream of water filled the first canteen. He replaced it with the second container and let the water pour into it.

Owen offered the full canteen to Yara, but she cast him an uneasy glance. He understood her hesitation, and only then realized he had grown to trust the magician. Her brother had died at the hands of the Wizard Rebellion, just as his own mother had.

Owen smiled at her and took a long draw of the water. The coolness refreshed his entire body. He couldn't remember ever tasting water so pure. "It's all right. I've learned a lot the past two days, and I have plenty to tell you. What are you doing here anyway?"

She cast him an indignant look. "You're welcome."

"Oh, sorry. Thank you for saving us back there. I'm glad you're here, but why did you come? And how did you find us?"

"I came because you didn't even tell me you were leaving, and I figured you'd need my help."

"I take full responsibility for leaving without telling you, Yara," Cedric said. "We had to leave quickly and with as few people knowing our destination as possible. But I, too, am curious how you found us."

"I left Innes Village as soon as I heard what happened. How did I find you? Ha! Did you mean to conceal your trail? I could smell the smoke from your fire last night, faint, but enough to sense your direction. I traveled as far as I could, but the dark forest floor made walking treacherous. I set out again early this morning and found your camp. It looked like I must not have missed you by much. I stayed on a path due west, and when the trees cleared, I could see you on the horizon. When I heard the fire hounds, I climbed onto the rocky cliffs to avoid them. They prefer low ground, you know?"

Owen surveyed the terrain as the sun sank below the horizon. The bright star appeared again over the western horizon just before the sun vanished. "I think we should camp here. We can't travel too much farther without evoking another fire hound attack. We can clean some of these fire hounds for food, and the remains should ward off another attack. Fire hounds avoid the smell of their own dead."

Cedric dropped his bag and staff and sat. He looked more exhausted than he had all day. "Let's hope that's true. I have no doubt under normal conditions fire hounds would stay away, but this attack had no resemblance of normal. A typical pack consists of five; sometimes one or two more will join, but have you ever heard of pack containing more than seven? I counted fifteen here."

Cedric set up camp while Owen and Yara prepared the meat. With no firewood present, Cedric conjured a magical fire. When Owen gutted the first beast, his injured shoulder gave a dull yelp of pain as the cutting motion aggravated the wound administered by Edward's sword. The metallic smell of the creature's blood filled the air.

Yara gagged. "What a stink!"

"Yeah," Owen said, "I remember it stank, but I haven't hunted with Father for years. I forgot how *bad* fire hounds smell. Be thankful. This smell may save our lives tonight."

"How many do we need to clean?"

"Probably most of them. They're wiry little animals without much meat. We can probably each eat one tonight."

Yara wrinkled her nose.

"Don't worry. They taste better than they smell. And I know a technique to cure the meat. So we can take some in our packs if we have enough salt. I have some."

"I brought some too." Yara glanced toward Cedric, who was far out of earshot. "So tell me about your new friend here. Do you trust him?"

"I don't know. I think so. At least I'm starting to trust him. We've talked a lot the past two days. I've learned a lot—about him *and* about the Wizard Rebellion."

Yara took a fire hound from the ground, slid her knife in its lower belly, and cut up to its neck, the rib bones cracking as the sharp blade passed through them. She stuck her hand in the cavity and pulled out a handful of guts and cast them aside. She turned her head and gasped for air. When she caught her breath, she continued, "I've never loathed Cedric on a personal level, as you have, but I have shared your distrust for magic and the Rebellion. I'm confident of your opinion of people, though, and if you believe in him, I think I can."

Owen told Yara most of what Cedric had told him as they cleaned the fire hounds and scattered the remains in a great circle surrounding their campsite. With each carcass they cleaned, they grew less sensitive to the smell.

After supper, Cedric used magic to form the fire hound skins into suitable water-skins and filled them.

Owen watched the bright star slowly sail east. Finally he asked Cedric, "What can you tell me about the attack at Innes Castle by the Wizard Rebellion? And what about my mother's death? If the Rebellion didn't come to Innes looking for you, why did they come?"

"Argnam came to persuade King Kendrick to give the Central Domain's support to the Rebellion. He knew the king would never support them, so he fully intended to use force in his persuasion.

"Six years had passed from the day your father rescued me from the desert. I have no idea what took Argnam so long to strike, but I have a guess. He didn't have many more supporters at the time of the attack than he had six years earlier. I think he became frustrated with his lack of allies, and instead of a well calculated move, he tried an all-or-nothing approach, not unlike your fighting style in yesterday's tournament, Owen."

Yara smiled and jabbed at his ribs.

Owen scowled. He didn't care for his fighting style being likened to a wizard's, especially the specific attack that killed his mother, but he didn't interrupt the story.

"I met your mother soon after my arrival at Innes Castle. Beatrix had a strong desire to learn magic. She had already taught herself a great deal about stargazing. Although stargazing has nothing to do with magic, for some reason, most people who learn stargazing often learn magic."

"By stargazing, you mean making predictions about what will happen based on the movements of the stars?" Yara asked.

"Yes. It's a tedious task that never appealed to me. It doesn't appeal to many people, for that matter. Too much vague interpretation, and often prophecies and predictions based on the stars prove false."

A fire hound howled in the distance, and Cedric raised his staff in the air. It glowed with a brilliant light, illuminating a substantial distance in all directions. No living fire hounds appeared, and no eyes shown in the dark beyond the dome of light. He continued the story.

* * * *

Cool wind whistled through the ramparts, and the flag atop the tallest tower fluttered so fast it became a blur. Occasional clouds sailed past, obscuring the moon for a few moments before passing by, but these small clouds were nothing more than scouts for the pending storm. Standing atop the lookout tower of Innes Castle, Cedric practiced a telescoping enchantment which made objects appear five times closer than their true location. From his standpoint, the moon took up a large portion of the night sky before him.

"Cedric," said a winded and worried voice from behind. "Cedric, I need... Oh, my!"

Cedric turned to see Beatrix, wide eyed, mouth agape, staring at the moon. He waved his hand, and the moon shrank to its original size. "Nothing to fear, Beatrix, just an enchantment."

She turned from the moon to Cedric. Fear still filled her eyes, and tears formed a thin, shiny rim around them. Too drastic of a reaction for seeing an enlarged moon.

She blinked and a tear fell from her left eye. "I need your help. It concerns stargazing. I know how you feel about it, but you have to hear this. Maybe if I say it aloud, I will see places where my interpretation failed, or maybe you can find a mistake in my reasoning."

"Go on then." Although he didn't put his faith in stargazing, he didn't want to discourage his pupil of six years. Her apprenticeship neared its end. He would have to give her an Endeavor soon. And if she could combine stargazing with her excellent powers as a sorceress, he could see no limit to what she may achieve.

"Have you notice the bright star that rises in the west just before sunset and progresses east until dawn?"

He nodded.

"I remember first noticing that star almost twelve years ago, just after Owen's birth. I didn't think much of it at that time. I hadn't started studying the stars, and I just assumed I had never noticed it. A lot changes after the birth of a child. In many ways, the beauty of the world becomes clearer."

Cedric's hair and beard blew in the wind. He nodded. "I'll have to take your word for that."

"But I've checked all of my star guides, and none of them mention that particular star. And to make it even more bizarre, I overheard some travelers talking in Innes Village the other day. They hailed from the Northern Domain, and they spoke of the star, and how they had never noticed it until they crossed the border into the Central Domain."

"That certainly does sound strange," Cedric said.

"Stellar apparitions only visible in certain regions of the world exist. Often called distress stars because they typically precede major events, or tragedies, which transform that part of the world. The Central Domain has not experienced one for over a century. The solar history books of Wittatun mention a distress star over the Central Domain the year the warrior Matteo, King Kendrick's great-great-grandfather, raised a secret army to overthrow the tyranny of Lord Outram.

"If this star truly did appear with the birth of my son, I fear what it represents. A specific type of distress star, Rector Parvulus, appears with the birth of a *child king*. I worry that Kendrick's life may be in danger."

Cedric thought for a moment. "I don't think you have anything to worry about. If this star is a Rector Parvulus, as you suspect, Owen could not be named king unless Kendrick names him heir to the throne. And he cannot do that for at least another three years."

\* \* \* \*

Owen stared at the bright star approaching its zenith. "That's the Rector Parvulus star she saw. I've always had a fondness for it, but I didn't know it had any kind of relationship to me."

Cedric looked at the star. "It may be a Rector Parvulus, or it may be some other astronomical anomaly. Unfortunately, with stargazing, one never knows for certain until after events have passed."

"But you've had your fifteenth birthday," Yara said. "You're no longer a child. You aren't the king. You're not even the legal heir to the throne, so that star must have a different meaning."

"If only stargazing followed human laws," Cedric said, remorsefully. "The Law of the Land says that Owen is no longer a child, but the celestial bodies follow their own laws. He could still fill the role of a child according to prophecy. King Kendrick never named his heir, and if he dies now, the consequences would far outweigh those of having such a young king."

Owen looked away from the star and fixed his gaze on Cedric. "But how does this relate to the Rebellion's attack at Innes Castle?"

"A few days after the evening on the watchtower, the Wizard Rebellion fell upon Innes Castle."

\* \* \* \*

The night sky lit up with bursts of red, blue, green, and yellow like a celebration of fireworks. Shadows appeared, danced across the ground, and vanished into the returning darkness. Cold rain fell, drenching the fighters' cloaks. Their feet splashed and slipped in puddles that had formed throughout the castle grounds from the two days of continuous rainfall. Cedric leaned out from behind a statue and sent magic of his own toward two veiled wizards standing in the courtyard. Their bodies fell limp and splashed on the wet ground.

Beatrix stood from the shelter she had taken behind a fallen pillar. "Thanks, Cedric. They had me trapped."

"Has someone taken the king to safety?" he asked, not wanting to waste time with idle talk.

"Yes," she said, "a young solder named Brahma came and took him to the inner chamber where he could direct the King's Sentry."

"Beatrix, I think the time has come for your Endeavor. Only two of the wizards here merit our attention. Argnam and his second in command, Necrose. If they fall, the Rebellion falls. I will take down Argnam. Your Endeavor is to stop Necrose."

They split-up, and Cedric found Argnam trying to break into the inner chamber, which served as King Kendrick's bunker and situation room.

Argnam turned at the sound of Cedric's footsteps. His hand glowed blue, and a sphere of light shot from it toward his former apprentice. The younger sorcerer dodged it, and the magic hit and destroyed the wall. Cedric charged his staff as he dove. When he landed, he rolled to his feet and launched the staff at Argnam. It penetrated the wizard, dead center of the chest, and exploded. Pieces of the staff, and of the wizard, flew in all directions. Cedric briefly remembered a dream from years past. He shook his head to clear the old thought before he sought Beatrix to aid her in battle with Necrose.

<u>CHAPTER SEVEN</u>

# Into Death Desert

The evening breeze blew cool, in total contrast to the mounting heat of the day.

Owen looked at the star now well on its way to the eastern horizon. "We'll have to sleep soon. I imagine tomorrow will take a lot out of us, traveling through the desert."

Cedric poked the blue flames of the magical fire with the end of his staff. The strange activity had the same effect of poking a fire made of burning wood. The flames grew taller, and the heat radiated more intensely to the campers. "This story nears its end, anyway. I didn't remember the specifics of my dream all those years ago until the next day when I had a chance to survey the aftermath of the battle. Never again have I seen the future in a dream."

Cedric placed his staff by his feet. "After I killed Argnam, I sought Beatrix. I found her in the courtyard almost exhausted from battle. Necrose looked even worse. Before I had a chance to intervene, they cast a set of spells toward each other. One hit a stone bench at Necrose's feet. It exploded, sending Necrose sailing over the wall of Innes Castle. I assumed her dead, but we never found her body. We even dragged a net through the moat, but it came up empty."

Owen readied himself for the rest of the story. He didn't know if he could tolerate Cedric recounting the death of his mother.

"The other spell hit Beatrix square in the chest." Cedric stopped and looked at Owen. "She fell to the ground and lay motionless. I ran to her and examined her, but I knew in my heart the truth before she even hit the ground. I realize it doesn't mean anything to you, Owen, but in my mind, she died with her Endeavor complete. She stopped Necrose. Your mother died a sorceress."

Owen kicked some pebbles into the fire, causing blue sparks to fly in all directions. "I remember that night. When I heard explosions, I grabbed my sword and left my quarters. At first I thought it was thunder, but the moon shone brightly through my window. I avoided a member of the King's Sentry. I heard him asking a chambermaid where to find me, so I ducked into a vacant room until he passed."

He paused to collect his thoughts. His head swam with memories and emotions. "I fled through the Great Hall into the courtyard. I saw Mother and Necrose fighting. I hid behind a statue and waited for an opportunity to strike. When I saw my chance, I tried to move, but my legs wouldn't listen." His head hung with shame over the memory. "I stood as motionless as the statue. I guess I was frozen by fear. I saw you run past. Then you watched as they both died."

"No, fear didn't keep you from jointing the battle," Cedric said. "I did. I came up behind you and saw what you intended. I cast an immobilizing spell at you. A boy armed with a sword would have gotten killed in that battle."

Owen stood and kicked the stone where he had sat. Pain shot up his leg, increasing the fury he felt toward Cedric as he stomped off into the shadows. *He used magic on me. That no good, sorry excuse for…and all this time I thought I was a coward. A foolish, childish coward!* He had fought every battle—whether in training or for real—since then to prove to himself he wasn't callow, or worse, craven, but deep inside, he always believed he was.

He fingered the hilt of his sword. How vindictive would it feel to run the blade all the way to the finger guard into Cedric's chest? But he knew he needed the magician to survive Death Desert. And a growing part of him knew the older man did what he felt was best for everyone.

He returned to the fire, and the three sat in silence for a while.

"Brahma was my brother," Yara said at last. "He died that night. We were told he took King Kendrick to safety before he died while pulling two wounded members of the Sentry clear of the battle. He received a Medal of Courage posthumously. My father accepted the honor but resigned his post as weaponsmith to the King's Sentry. We moved from

Innes Castle to Innes Village, and he set up a private smithy. He couldn't bear to live at the castle any longer."

Owen felt like a fool for his earlier rant. Had he completely forgotten that Yara suffered a loss too? And what about the other dead members of the Sentry? Many of them were fathers and husbands. He put a hand on Yara's shoulder and gave a soft squeeze. Not knowing what to say to her, he stood, stretched, and found a smooth patch of ground to spread his pack. "We need to get our sleep."

* * * *

The next day, the sun rose with the intensity of dragon's fire. No sooner had it broken the horizon when Owen woke from the heat. He didn't speak as they packed their belongings, his blood returning to a boil over the end of Cedric's story from the night before. Cedric had admitted to sending Beatrix to her death. More than that, the magician stopped him from assisting. Yet part of him knew his mother would have had it no other way. He sighed with resignation. At least his mother had defeated Necrose, possibly saving King Kendrick. Not that he would trade his mother's life for his father's, or the other way around, but the Central Domain could not survive without a king.

Yara tried to catch his eye, but he looked away. *She's probably furious with me about how I acted last night, and here I am dwelling on it again.*

When Cedric had gained some ground on them, Yara walked close to Owen. "Are you all right, Owen? You seem distant."

He walked silently for several paces. "I don't know. I understand why Cedric never told me about his role in my mother's death before. I wouldn't have accepted it. Now that I've come to trust him…" He realized what he said and amended it, "At least somewhat, I'm not sure what to think." He cast a sideways glace at her. "And I feel bad for focusing on my problems, and forgetting your brother died also."

"I'll tell you what I think. My brother and your mother did their duty to the kingdom. And I don't know of anything more noble."

Owen supposed Yara was right, but knowing his mother died for a noble cause did little to lessen the sting of her loss.

With each step, the desert became hotter. The heat created what appeared to be wavy, transparent plants, which sprouted from the ground and grew at least as tall as a castle tower. Owen's dragon-mail armor allowed air to pass to his torso, but his legs and feet dripped with sweat. Yara appeared more comfortable in her lighter clothing, and somehow Cedric didn't look hot at all in his robes.

"Why doesn't this heat bother you?" Owen asked him.

"Magic." Cedric smiled. He raised a hand toward Owen and Yara. A chill like a winter gale blasted them head on. He felt the sweat on his legs freeze. The magician stopped, and the desert heat came on full again.

"Don't you freeze?" Owen asked.

"I don't use as much on myself. Using magic tires a person. I just use it enough to keep the heat from killing me…well, us. I've been using it on you and Yara as well. Just a little. I didn't tell you. I didn't want to upset you."

"You mean this heat," Yara said, holding up her arms as if she could support the heat, "isn't even the full intensity of the desert?"

Cedric chuckled. "No. Without magic, a person would have trouble getting this far into Death Desert."

They passed several stone formations with varying shapes. Some looked like skulls, others more closely resembled buildings. Cedric explained a theory that stated the hot barren land of Death Desert may once have been an ocean, and the water carved the rocks.

Soon they came to a herd of emmoths. Owen had never hunted emmoths. His father occasionally did, but he had never accompanied him, not seeing the sport in hunting such a large, slow, and clumsy creature. Now seeing living emmoths for the first time, he understood the attraction. It had the face of a boar and the body of an elephant. A tusk as long as one of its legs protruded from either side of its lower jaw, while two smaller tusks hung from the top jaw like ivory stalactites.

He knew the method for hunting them. A hunter would sneak up on the beast, climb its back, and slit its throat. The whole time, the creature would thrash about, trying to dislodge the attempted slayer.

Cedric advised them to remain quiet and move slowly, so as not to draw the attention of the emmoths. But when Owen thought the emmoths had decided not to bother with the three of them, the ground shook. Behind them, an emmoth charged. Its head flung from side to side. Its tusks tore through the hard, dry ground as if it were soft mud.

Owen drew his sword, Cedric raised his staff, and Yara tried to nock an arrow to her bow string, but none of them had time to mount a defense. They jumped out of the way just before the tusks tore past them. Owen rolled to his knees in time to see Cedric's leg get crushed by the emmoth. Even over the thundering hooves, he could hear the crunch of bones and his scream of agony.

On his left, a different emmoth galloped toward him. The one that had trampled Cedric skidded to a stop and turned back toward them. Then both emmoths charged.

From Cedric's direction, an orange beam of light flew and hit one emmoth. Its legs stopped moving, and it fell on its face. It slid to a stop before it collided with Owen.

"Owen, behind you!" warned Yara.

He turned to see Cedric running toward him. Impossible! His leg had shattered! Another orange beam shot over his right shoulder. Two arrows flew in rapid succession from Yara's bow. He spun, expecting to see another emmoth fall. Instead, he saw a flash of white as an emmoth's tusk plunged into his stomach. Dark spots marred his vision until Death Desert faded into blackness...

Owen, Cedric, and Yara stood in a dark cave. The path split in two, and Owen had to decide which direction to take. At some point, Yara vanished. The ground faded, and he fell through. The room he landed in had black walls that wriggled. That didn't make sense, but his senses were scrambled. He wanted to find Yara, needed to find her, but Cedric told him he couldn't. He didn't think he could leave her, yet he knew he could not find her. The walls faded and reformed, and a new room opened before him. A pedestal stood in the center, and a white dragon shown bright with its own emitted light. The pain of a thousand fires filled Owen's right hand.

The room, the dragon, and the pain faded. Death Desert returned with the sweltering sun again ablaze in the sky. Yara stood, and Cedric knelt with his hand on Owen's stomach. A huge emmoth tusk, his dragon-mail, and tunic lay next to him.

Owen looked down to see his chest and stomach covered with blood but detected no mark of a wound anywhere. His stomach felt uneasy, but it didn't hurt.

Cedric stood. "There, I think you'll find a magically healed stomach more desirable than one impaled with an emmoth tusk."

Owen looked around, confused. "Where did you take me? And where did you find Yara?"

"What?" Cedric asked.

"*I* found *you* yesterday," Yara said. "What do you mean by where did Cedric find me? I'll tell you, though, I thought you were lost for a while there."

Owen closed his eyes to stop the sun for a moment. He couldn't think in the bright light. "I need some water." After taking a long draw from a water-skin, he was able to speak. "The three of us entered a cave. I'm not sure where it was now. I did know; I just can't remember. Something happened to you, Yara. I don't know. You were there, then gone." He raised his right hand and flexed it before his face. "Something happened to my hand, but it's fine now."

"That all happened in your mind," Cedric said. "We came upon the emmoths, and one nearly killed you. Yara shot a few, but arrows don't do much to emmoth skin. I scared the rest away."

"You should have seen it," Yara added. "He made all these lights shoot from his staff. It looked like fireworks."

Cedric waved a hand at her. "I just used some light trickery developed by a now ancient magician named Vivek. He made quite a name for himself with it. This was a time predating magic persecution. But his story is for another day."

Owen rubbed a hand across his belly. Healing was the most common use for magic. But since he tried not to think about magic, he didn't realize how powerful the healing could be. Wounds like Cedric's leg and his stomach would have been beyond the power of the most skilled traditional healers. "You mended your leg and my stomach. How?"

"With magic."

"No, I mean *how* did you do it." He paused as the words stuck in his throat. "I have to learn magic."

"Me too," Yara added.

Cedric smiled. "I think you will both make excellent apprentices. Stand up, Owen."

He didn't think he could stand after taking an emmoth tusk to the gut, but he tried and stood with ease. The magician knelt and picked up four small stones, handing Owen and Yara two each.

"Place a stone on either side of your palm." They did as instructed. "Now concentrate as hard as you can on the stones, and move them together with your mind."

Owen did as instructed, even though he had no idea how to concentrate on such an activity.

Nothing happened.

Cedric beamed at them. "There! Very good. Just like that."

Owen looked to see if Yara had done something he hadn't. Her stones still rested on her palm and a confused expression rested on her face.

"What do you mean 'just like that'?" Owen asked. "They didn't move."

"No, but you were concentrating well. Do it again."

He made another attempt, and another, and another. He continued to try the rest of the daylight hours as they traveled across the desert. Though Cedric praised Yara for her effort, her stones also stayed stationary.

They didn't come across any more emmoths, or any other wildlife for that matter, and they had nothing better to do than work on moving the pebbles while the experienced magician used magic to keep them from dying in the heat.

That evening, they stopped to make camp.

"I'm glad you dried some fire hound meat last night, Owen," Cedric said. "Otherwise we'd be going without food tonight. No living creature resides this far into Death Desert. We entered the Western Domain some time ago."

Owen handed some dried meat to Yara and Cedric. "I think fire hound always tastes better the second day, anyway."

As night set in, the cloudless sky lost all its heat and the air became cool again. Cedric, for a second time, used magic to make a fire. Owen would have never imagined they would need a fire this night after the heat of the day, but as he held the pebbles in his hand, his fingertips started to numb from the cold.

Owen and Yara sat on a large boulder, staring at their pebbles. Cedric rested across from them, watching. Very subtly, and only someone paying close attention would have noticed, the pebbles in Yara's hand twitched.

"Cedric! Did you see that?" she asked.

"Yes, good work. How are you doing, Owen?"

Owen thought he would quit for the night. He had never tried so hard for something only to fail. Then his pebbles moved as well. He looked at Cedric to see him beaming with excitement.

"I knew the two of you would make excellent apprentices. When Argnam handed me two pebbles, it took me the good part of a week to get them to move like that. And now, I think we should get our rest."

Owen put the pebbles on the ground and looked at his surroundings for the first time in a long while. The western sky glowed red, and no star appeared on the horizon. He didn't know if the red light blocked out the star, but he had a suspicion the star was gone.

"What is causing that light?" he asked.

"That's where we're headed," Cedric said. "The Land of Fire."

# CHAPTER EIGHT

# The Land of Fire

Owen didn't sleep well that night. Each time he'd fall asleep, dreams about the dark cave assaulted him. Channels of magma flowed through endless corridors. It appeared Owen, Cedric, and Yara were the only ones there, but he felt the presence of another creature or creatures. The dreams always ended near the white dragon. His hand would scream with pain just before he saw the dragon. He'd wake clutching his hand, unsure if the screams were real or in his dream.

Also making it difficult to sleep was the fact that it never got much darker than dusk. The western sky flashed and flickered with explosions. Occasionally, a flame shot into the air from just over the horizon.

When Owen finally got some rest, he awoke to find the sun had risen. Cedric was packing their camp. He groaned, realizing he wouldn't have a chance at anymore sleep.

Owen picked his dragon-mail armor off the ground. A huge hole penetrated the stomach. The armor failed in its first true test, at least since it fell into Owen's possession, but he felt compelled to take it, as it had passed through generations in his family. He pulled the lightweight armor over his tunic with a matching hole, Cedric took up his staff, and Yara slung her bow and quiver over her shoulders.

Seeing the staff made Owen think of something he hadn't considered before. "Cedric? What is the purpose of your staff? Last night, when we learned to move the stones, you said all someone has to do is concentrate to use magic. Yet I've seen you use your staff for magic."

Cedric gazed at the staff thoughtfully. "The staff is no more, and no less, than a tool. I can perform all the traditional magic I know, healing people and directing energy, simply through determination of my mind, but I can use the staff to make it more powerful."

Owen frowned at him.

"Imagine a hammer. You can push a stake into the ground with your hands, but it's easier if you have a tool, such as a hammer."

Owen nodded, beginning to understand.

"Magic is similar but a little different. Traditional magic involves mental strength, not physical strength. A staff serves as a focal point. When a sorcerer concentrates on the staff, the magic becomes more powerful. That's why magicians teach stone moving first. You used the stones as your focal point. Non-traditional magic, such as potions, sacrificial magic, and so many other things it would take me at least a day just to list them all, differs, but sometimes it needs a focal point too."

"So you don't need your staff to perform any traditional magic?" Yara asked.

"No, but without it, I think we would have had a bit more trouble with those emmoths yesterday." Cedric let out a little chuckle, though Owen cringed to think of the tusk embedded in his stomach.

They walked toward the fire. The sun rose higher, but they appeared to stay fixed in the same spot, regardless of how far they progressed. The desert terrain never changed; the Land of Fire stayed in the distance.

The two novices mastered moving the stones in their palms. Soon, they could move the stones to each other's palms without much effort.

Still hours from midday, Owen could feel his skin starting to singe. He tried to shield his head with his arms to block the intense heat. In the distance, visions of mountains, cities, and oceans formed in the heat mirages, but regardless of how far they walked, the visions stayed the same distance from them.

Cedric shot them with a blast of cool air. "I think it's time you two learn some more magic. Try to concentrate on the cold. Imagining a winter storm may help."

Owen tried, but with the intense heat, winter eluded him, a tale from legends. He couldn't imagine anything cooler than his own body, impaled by a skewer, over an open flame.

Yara's hair had come out of its ponytail and clung to her face, darkened with sweat. No success for her, either.

"Try again," Cedric said. "This is no more difficult than moving the stones. You just have a larger focal point. Concentrate first on your head and move down your body."

Owen tried again. This time, he thought of falling headfirst into a snow bank as a small boy. He remembered the snow falling down the neck of his coat, freezing him to the bone. Once he lost himself in the memory, he didn't feel so hot anymore. He didn't feel cold but definitely cooler than a moment earlier.

"I'm doing it!" Owen said excitedly.

Cedric pointed his staff at Owen. "Keep practicing and here's what you'll be able to do." The air froze as a blue mass raced toward Owen. The hot desert became frozen tundra.

That same winter he had remembered from his childhood, he tried to walk across a frozen stream. In the middle, the ice cracked. He fell into the freezing water up to his waist. Even as cold as the water made him, it barely compared with Cedric's magic.

Drops of liquid fell from the staff head, but unlike the water they collected in the fire hound skins, these drops evaporated into a cloud of steam before they even hit the hot desert ground.

Cedric lowered his staff, and Owen immediately started warming. Two days ago, having magic used on him would have infuriated him. Now it left him wondering if he would really be able to perform it as well someday.

Yara didn't seem to have the talent with this magic as she did with moving the stones, but she urged them to continue on to the Land of Fire instead of waiting all day for her to learn the skill.

Owen kept himself cool enough to bear the heat, but nowhere near as cold as Cedric had made him. Sometimes, when he could lose himself in thought, he would truly make himself cold, not just cool. He and Cedric took turns cooling Yara until she exclaimed that she could cool herself.

Yara's lips formed a weary smile. "I didn't think I'd ever learn that one. I told myself I'd give up after two more failed tries, but it worked."

The ground changed from a dusty brown to a solid gray-black. Several mountains rose in the distance—real mountains this time, instead of mirages—with peaks of orange, not the white and blue of mountains in the Central Domain. Red rivers flowed down the mountain sides. Bursts of steam shot from the ground beneath everyone's feet. Not far ahead the land became a molten lake of fire.

They stopped at the edge of the land.

Owen looked at the vast pool of lava before them. "This must be the Land of Fire." He knew magic was the only thing making it possible to stand so close to it. But even with magic, incredible heat threatened to burn him.

Cedric wiped sweat from his brow. "I'm glad the two of you learned some magic. I'm not sure I have the power to protect three people from this heat. Follum lives in a cave in one of those volcanoes. We have to cross the lake to get there."

Owen looked doubtfully at Cedric. How did he expect them to cross a lake of lava?

"It's really no harder than what you've been doing to stay cool. You'll just have to cool the lava instead of yourself to make a spot to walk. Watch how I do it."

Cedric moved the tip of his staff toward the lava, which turned from red to black. Steam screamed from the newly formed rock, and the air filled with the odor of brimstone. He stepped onto the rock and moved his staff to a new point just ahead. The lava turned black, and he took another step.

As soon as his foot left the first patch of stone, it melted into lava again. "You'll have to move quickly."

Owen stepped to the edge and hesitated. He had done some magic, but nothing compared to this. If he left one patch too hot, he would sink. And this wouldn't be like the frozen stream he had fallen into as a child. As a child, he returned to the castle and warmed himself. This lake would give no second chances.

Cedric, now five or six steps ahead, turned back. "Use your sword as a focal point if you must. Yara, use an arrow."

Owen unsheathed his sword and pointed it at the lava. He concentrated on cooling it. The surface turned darker, steam hissed, and small pebble-sized rocks formed, but they melted as quickly as they formed. Yara tried. The lava darkened for her, but she didn't produce the solid chunks he could.

"What's taking so long?" Cedric shouted from far ahead.

Owen looked up to tell him he couldn't do it when the hem of Cedric's robes caught fire. Owen's mouth hung open as the magician moved on, seeming not to notice the flames all around him.

Without hesitating, Owen pointed his sword at Cedric and thought of winter in the mountains. In his mind, wind deafened him and blinded him with blowing snow. An avalanche raced toward him from the tallest peaks. Yara pointed her arrow. A faint blue mist coursed from the tip of the sword and arrow. It covered the lava all the way to the bottom of Cedric's robes, engulfing them. The fire died, and a path of solid stone formed in the lake. When they ceased their magic, the lake turned red again.

Cedric looked down at his singed robes. "Now can we get going?"

*He let himself catch fire on purpose. He could have died. How could he trust us, with our limited experience? That crazy old...*

The magician walked on, and Owen pointed his sword at the lava again. This time he had no problem causing the lava to freeze solid. Yara crossed at his side, making a path of her own. He cast her a questioning glance to see if she realized what Cedric had done. Growing up together, they could often communicate with nothing more than their eyes. She shook her head with a puzzled expression on her face. *She thinks he's crazy, too.*

By the midpoint of the lake, Owen thought his patches of solid rock may have been as large as Cedric's, but he didn't point it out. He didn't want to get distracted or to distract his friends. They were making good progress, but they still had a lot of lake to cross.

As they approached the western edge, the dark shadow of a person standing at the end of the lake impregnated the bright glow of the fire.

"I think someone's watching us, Cedric," Yara said.

"I've noticed him," Cedric said. "I believe my old friend Follum has come to greet us. Why he doesn't help us cross, I don't know."

They continued across the Lake of Fire. The man on the other end did not move. Owen wondered if he was alive, but at the same time, his skin prickled with the feeling the man watched him.

They neared the shore, and the old man raised his arms high before bringing them down in a flash. From his hands came the same blue mist Owen and Yara had made when Cedric caught fire. The lake froze solid all around them. Sulfur-smelling steam rose from the ground, choking them. The blue mist stopped, but the lake did not melt as fast as it did when the other two had frozen it. They hurried to the shore.

A man taller, and more muscular than Cedric, waited for them. He wore a robe similar to Cedric's but made of red fabric. His unadorned appearance, with short, white hair and no beard, made him look unremarkable. His only distinguishing features were the scars lining his hands and face. Although his body appeared fit and strong, his sunken eyes and wrinkled skin revealed an ancient man, much older than Cedric.

The man's red eyes darted to each of them in turn. "Do you come as friends or foes?"

Owen felt as if the man's gaze could actually examine him on some internal level.

"We come as friends," Cedric said. "Has the time of our parting been so vast that you have forgotten the face of a friend?"

"Of course I remember you, Cedric," Follum said, "but I do not know your companions. Terrible times have come for wizards." Owen started at the way Follum said "wizard" as if it wasn't a slur. "It is difficult to know who to trust. And we didn't part on the best terms. Why do you seek me now?"

"I bring the son of King Kendrick of the Central Domain. His father has fallen under a spell, and we need your help releasing him."

Follum gestured for them to follow him. "Please, come to my cavern. I try to keep myself out of the affairs of both man and wizard, but since you have come this far… How may I help you?"

"Cedric made a potion to save my father," Owen explained, "but it didn't work. He said he had never seen magic like it before. He hoped you might know of a magic that he doesn't."

Follum turned his head to address Cedric. "I assume you used a healing draught."

"Yes, but it did nothing. The king didn't even stir."

"I see." Follum stopped outside the entrance to a cavern, letting his visitors enter first. "A healing draught will cure any common poison, so long as the victim is not dead. Since you are here, I will assume your king is still alive."

The cavern was cool, damp, and completely different from the outside world. Stalagmites had been fashioned into furniture. Follum gestured for his visitors to be seated. Cedric and Yara sat, but Owen paced, waiting to hear if the old man recognized the magic.

Follum rested with his chin in his hands. "I have seen magic such as this before, but I don't know of any wizard still practicing it. Most magic is general; it works on everyone the same way. This is a more individualized magic. You will need to make a potion with an ingredient unique to your king."

Owen thought for a moment. "My father cared for the kingdom, for his armor collection, for me. None of these things could be made into a potion."

Cedric shook his head. "You're thinking too literally. We'll have to think symbolically to find the ingredient. Keep naming things that mean a lot to your father."

Owen stopped pacing, rested a hand on the cavern wall, and bowed his head to consider. "I've thought of everything. Oh, wait! Dragons! His family crest is a green dragon."

Follum snapped his fingers. "Now you're onto something. Dragons were a common theme in this type of magic. How did the poison enter your father's body? Mode of entry will also have a strong connection."

Owen pondered the question for a moment. "Just before he collapsed, when Father split the bread, a faint dust fell on his face. I think he may have inhaled it. I thought it was just crumbs, but maybe they contained poison...or magic."

Cedric wagered a guess. "Could it be Dragon's Breath?"

Follum nodded. "That sounds like the most logical choice."

"Do you have some here?" Owen asked, unfamiliar with Dragon's Breath.

Follum shook his head. "No. There's only one place to find Dragon's Breath, the snow caps of Ice Island."

Owen groaned. "Ice Island? It will take us a week to get there by sea. Maybe longer. At least winter hasn't started yet. We can still pass through the Northern Straits."

"How do we get there?" Yara wanted to know. "We haven't got a boat."

"Neither have I," Follum said. "You'll have to ride a dragon."

# CHAPTER NINE

# The Great-Dragon Riddle

At the mention of dragon riding, Owen looked at Yara. Her wide-eyed, open-mouthed expression told him the news of living dragons shocked her as well. Cedric didn't appear surprised. Many of Owen's beliefs had been tested on this journey, but the thought of living dragons seemed inconceivable. *Was this some joke between the two magicians?*

He watched for Follum's face to betray a lie. "I thought dragons went extinct."

One corner of Follum's mouth rose to a grin. "Dragons have *almost* gone extinct. Humans have hunted them for eons and have almost wiped them out. Please, take a seat and I will tell you the story of the Great-Dragon."

Owen realized he had started pacing again and sat on a stalagmite bench near Yara.

"In days of old, dragons covered the world," Follum began. "The few humans lived in small villages on the plains or in networks of caverns in the mountains. Humans and dragons rarely interacted. The dragons had plenty of land to roam, and the human villages did not interest them. Likewise, the humans left the dragons alone. Dragons did not pose a threat, and humans did not hunt them, as dragon meat is poisonous."

Owen knew all this and tapped his foot with impatience as he waited for Follum to get to the part about the living dragons.

"Eventually the human population grew, and people had to expand into areas inhabited by dragons. Dragons, in turn, defended their territory to protect their nests and eggs. When human numbers grew too great to combat, dragons went into hiding with the help of wizards and the Great-Dragon. You'll need to understand this story if you want to find a dragon."

Fire raged outside and flickered shadows on the walls. Owen, Yara, and Cedric sat in Follum's comfortable cave and listened to the story of the Great-Dragon unfold.

\* \* \* \*

A cool northern wind made the far northeast portion of Death Desert unlike the rest. Although rarely greeted with rain, the heat never became unbearable. The dry ground had more of a red, rocky appearance than the brown cracked dirt everywhere else. The wide, deep bed of a long since dried up river cut through the ground, leaving only rocky bluffs.

Two men, one no more than a teenager, the other old enough to be his grandfather, approached a large colorful creature resting between two large rocks. Their cloaks flapped in the wind, and the younger man pulled his tighter. As they neared the beast, its color changed with every step. Red, orange, yellow, chartreuse, green, blue, black, and purple all gleamed off its scales, evidently at the same time.

The younger man turned to his companion. "Follum, you say this dragon can speak? Better than most dragons, I mean."

"Yes, Argnam. Most dragons can only mimic the words we say, much like some birds. They do have limited understanding of the meaning of the words. This dragon can speak fluently. We call it the Great-Dragon because it has qualities of all the different breeds of dragons. Some people think it belongs to an otherwise extinct ancestral species that begat all other varieties. Whereas some others take their beliefs further, saying he predates all other dragons, and he and a now dead ancient female dragon parented all dragon species."

"What does the Great-Dragon say?"

"He's too old to recall his youth. He can remember a time before man, but all the other varieties of dragons already existed in his earliest memories."

The dragon must have noticed them coming. It raised its long head and stretched two massive leathery wings. The beast stood and arched its back. Spikes protruded in a ridge down its length, each as tall as a grown man. A tree trunk-sized tail swung out from under it, and a large, forked spike extended from the tip.

"Welcome, wizards," the Great-Dragon said. "I hear you discussing my age: a favored topic among humans. Have you prepared the magic I requested, Follum?"

"I have placed the task on Argnam, my apprentice. As one of the most gifted magicians I've ever trained, I thought the creation of a magic to hide dragons from the eyes of humans a fitting task for his Endeavor."

The Great-Dragon examined Argnam. Its glassy, red eyes looked like two enormous rubies. Only its pupils, tiny black dots in the center of each eye, moved. "Young, don't you think, even by human standards? You believe he's ready for his Endeavor?"

Follum nodded. "We would not have come if I did not have complete faith in his abilities."

"You'll get one chance at this, young one. A magic of this nature will only work with me, no other dragon. If you fail, humans will erase dragons from the planet. They want the healing properties of our blood, the strength of our scales for armor—no one has yet discovered a substance as hard as dragon bone—and they even take our eggs for good luck charms. The last is *clearly* dependent upon perspective."

Argnam bowed his head in a respectful manner to the timeworn creature. "I started studying sacrificial magic prior to Follum taking me as an apprentice. I won't disappoint you and the rest of the dragons."

The Great-Dragon turned and walked away. "It's time to proceed. Don't fret for my life. The time has come for me to move on from this world. Even without this sacrifice, I doubt I could live more than another year. Follow me into that cave in the bluff, youngling. I have reason to believe I was born here. I find it fitting that here I shall also die."

Argnam followed the Great-Dragon into the cave. It had told Follum only one wizard could attend the sacrifice, but knowing this made it no easier for the master to accept his powerlessness and remain inactive. A flash of light exploded from the cave mouth, and heaviness sank in Follum's chest. He knew, without a doubt, the dragon's life had ended. Now he could only wait.

And wait he did.

For over two days, Argnam remained concealed in the bluff. Follum watched the sky for dragons. He saw none, but that didn't confirm the magic had worked. Dragons never frequented this land. The cool air blowing in from the Northern Domain didn't create favorable conditions for the monstrous reptiles.

When Argnam exited the cavern, he appeared much older than when he had entered. Exhaustion streaked his face. Sweat matted his hair, and filth covered his robes. The first word that came to Follum's mind when he saw his now former apprentice: frail.

Argnam approached Follum and fell to his knees. "It's done."

From within his robes, he produced two weapons, a sword and a staff, both whiter than any substance Follum had ever seen, and by their appearance, fashioned from two bones of the Great-Dragon. He laid them at Follum's feet.

A mist arose from the ground. First pure white, then silver, it became as large as the Great-Dragon before taking on his shape. The spirit of the Great-Dragon surveyed the wizards, and the two relics made from his bones.

"Your apprentice succeeded, Follum," the spirit said. "The relics before you—the Dragon Sword and the Dragon Staff—represent the only way humans can contact dragons henceforth. The wielder of one can tame the dragon; the wielder of both can become the dragon."

The relics faded and disappeared. Follum looked from the spirit to Argnam and back again.

"I have hidden the relics in two separate locations in Wittatun," the Great-Dragon's spirit said. "Anyone seeking a dragon must first find a relic. Only I know their location, but Argnam has enchanted them with magic to protect them in their hiding place."

"But how do we find them?" Follum asked.

"By solving a portion of this riddle," the spirit said.

*Twin rivers of fire, below them go*
*For sword you seek, and flame you will know.*
*Beneath the fire, two sloping paths lead*
*Take not the one protected by steed.*

*Where ground steps soft, and pungent air may burn,*
*The Dragon Staff creates your yearn.*
*Wade through the marsh, find two caves buried there.*

*Select the path guarded by mare.*

*Second into the fire maze,*
*Should seize the sword or feel the blaze.*
*And for the staff I must speak true,*
*The first one near will not turn blue.*

*If sword then shadow you must defeat.*
*If staff then death you'll have to beat.*
*And if, indeed, us both you gain,*
*We'll mend your injuries and pain.*

After reciting the riddle, the Great-Dragon paused to give them time to mull it over. "A time may come when humans need the aid of dragons. These relics will ensure dragons live long enough to provide that assistance. They will also provide a portal through the magic shield defending my kind, making dragons accessible, and vulnerable, to man."

A northern gust of wind blew cold. The spirit of the Great-Dragon lost its misty form and was swept away in the current.

\* \* \* \*

Owen removed his dragon-mail armor. He sat, holding it and thinking of the dragon that must have died, thereby surrendering its skin and scales to make the armor. Shame overflowed in him for something which used to fill him with pride.

He walked to the mouth of the cave and tossed the dragon-mail as far as he could. A dull pain shot through his shoulder from what remained of the stab wound he received from Edward's sword in the tournament. Absently, he touched the wound and used magic to heal it. The pain vanished. He looked at it in surprise. No scar of the cut remained.

"Impressive," Cedric said.

Owen looked at him. "I didn't even think about what I did. It just happened."

"Yes," Cedric said. "One needs a powerful mind to perform magic, but the mind often serves as the hindrance of magic: the magician's paradox."

Owen stared west at a land he had never seen before today, lost in thought. "So we'll need to find one of the relics, and in turn, find a dragon?"

"Precisely," Follum said.

"What did The Great-Dragon mean by, 'The wielder of both can become the dragon'?" Owen asked.

"It's hard to say, but he didn't literally mean that someone could turn into a dragon. That's impossible, but a person could *appear* as a dragon at times. Or, what is most likely, the wielder could get the protective powers of the dragon. That is how I interpret the last line of the riddle."

Cedric stood next to Owen. "But the location of both relics does not affect our journey. We need only one in order to find a dragon to take us to Ice Island."

Follum joined the two other men at the entrance of the cave. The sun set precisely between two volcanoes in the distance. Again the absence of the bright star rising in the west gave Owen an eerie sensation. When the sun dipped below the horizon, the two volcanoes glowed reddish-orange as rivers of lava flowed down them.

Owen pointed at the volcanoes. "That's where we have to go, isn't it? Those are the twin rivers from the riddle."

Yara rushed over to see what the three men spoke of.

"I believe so," Follum said. "I have never looked for it myself, but the riddle seems clear that one relic rests here, in the Inferno, while the other resides in the swamplands in the Southern Domain."

"I think Argnam certainly believed the swamp held the Dragon Staff," Cedric said. "He never told me of the relics, but he always had a base of operations near the swamp. I don't suspect he ever found the Dragon Staff. If he had, he would have used it the night the Rebellion attacked Innes Castle."

Cedric turned to Follum. "We'll rest here tonight, if that's all right with you."

Follum nodded. "You'll need all your strength once you get to the Inferno. At least two wizards have died trying to obtain the Dragon Sword."

Hearing Follum use the word 'wizard' sparked a question in Owen. "Follum, why do you so freely use the term wizard? I mean, you use magic, and the term has such a hateful, derogatory connotation."

"Words change meaning over time," Follum said. "I don't concern myself with the current meanings of words any more than I worry about the affairs of wizards and men. The term 'wizard' is not hateful; the ignorant person calling a magic user 'wizard' is hateful."

"So, you think of yourself as a wizard?"

"I am a wizard. I have been a wizard for over ninety years, and I will continue to be a wizard until the day I die."

Satisfied with the answer, but unsure if he agreed with Follum's conviction, Owen dropped the subject.

Yara took up the conversation. "How old are you, Follum?"

Follum laughed and returned to his seat. "I'm not old, child, just experienced. Wizards can stretch a few more years out of life than someone without magic—if they don't get killed. I've been around for over one-hundred and five years. I took my Endeavor at the tender age of fifteen. The youngest wizard in history, I believe. Even younger than Argnam and the great wizard Vivek. I hope to live another twenty or thirty years before I pass to the World of Enchantment."

As night fell, Follum fed his visitors and gave them bedding. Owen welcomed the change of sleeping indoors on something that resembled a bed.

Owen's rest was again filled with horrors. Dreams of Innes Castle. A storm bellowed outside. His green robes, like a sorcerer's, clung to him from the rain. He had to find his father. He needed to give him something. *What?* Owen couldn't remember, but he never needed to give his father anything more important.

His surroundings changed. Magicians garded all gates to the castle. *Has Father replaced the King's Sentry with magicians? Impossible!*

The courtyard faded, and now he stood in a hallway. Outside the King's Chamber, someone lay on the ground before him. Owen stepped closer to investigate. *Is he dead?*

## CHAPTER TEN

# Twin Rivers of Fire

Owen cradled the dead man in his arms, but the dead man behaved strangely. Raising an arm, he started jabbing Owen in the ribs. Owen tried to put the body down, but he couldn't move. The dream faded, and he awoke to a dull poking from Cedric's staff. The shock of waking all but erased the dream from his mind.

Owen propped himself on weak, tingly arms. "What?"

Cedric stopped prodding him. "Wake up! We have to leave, now."

Owen rubbed his eyes, still groggy from interrupted sleep. "What's happening?"

Yara packed her belongings on the opposite side of the cave. Cedric and Follum paced while the younger two readied themselves. Outside the cave, the black western sky still shown with stars.

Cedric walked to the opening and faced toward the volcanoes. "A storm approaches."

"Okay, I've seen storms before," Owen said.

"Not like this," Cedric said. "I think magic called this tempest."

Owen peered out the door of the cave. "I see a clear night sky."

He searched for his dragon-mail armor before remembering he had disposed of it. Follum handed him a folded garment. Owen spread it open, revealing a green robe not unlike those which Cedric and Follum wore. A memory of his dream, just a glimpse, flashed into his mind but faded before he could grasp it.

"Green is the color of King Kendrick's family, if I'm not mistaken," Follum said. "This is the only green robe I have, but you are welcome to take it, since you seem to have lost some of your apparel."

"Thank you," Owen said. What surprised him most, he meant it.

The robe contained many pockets and even secret pockets inside other pockets. He had no trouble moving the contents of his knapsack to the robe. Before he put the cursed collar in a pocket, he thought about his new friendship with Cedric. *How different will life be when we revive Father and return to our normal lives?*

With their possessions packed, they set out for the western edge of Wittatun as a band of four. Follum led the way with Cedric. The two experienced magicians lit their staffs, illuminating their passage over the rocky terrain. The predawn air grew hot and sticky from the surrounding lava and geysers.

The apprentices practiced what magic they knew. Owen continued to find it easier to use magic if he kept his mind from trying too hard.

To his left, Yara touched the tip of an arrow. It glowed a faint red in the early twilight. She loosed it at a pile of rocks. When it struck, the rocks exploded as if an entire bag of black powder had detonated.

The firelight and the glow from the staffs highlighted the amusement in Cedric's eyes. "For two people who had no intention of ever learning magic a few days ago, you have become quick learners."

They approached the western shore, and the ocean looked calm and glassy. The sky behind them became purple and pink with the returning sun. A strait passed between the continental mainland and the distant islands where the twin volcanoes rose. The western sky now appeared starless. The eastern sky brightened. A faint outline of dark clouds emerged, signifying the storm to come.

Owen caught up with Cedric. "How did you know a storm approached before now?"

"Haven't you learned that those in touch with magic are likewise more in touch with the environment?" Cedric asked.

A sharp slope led to the shore of the strait. Follum motioned for the other three to scale it to the shore. He removed a conch shell from the pocket of his robe and blew two great bellows.

As they descended to the sea, two immense jets of mist erupted from the strait, and the noise of the conch returned from a distant creature.

Owen pointed. "I think I see an animal."

Follum caught up with them in their descent. "Yes. A leviathan. It will carry you across the strait. Leviathans are the oldest living creatures."

"Even older than dragons?" Yara asked.

"Much older," Follum said.

The leviathan swam toward them, winding from side to side like a snake. Occasionally it would propel its massive body into the air and submerge, making a series of arches.

The first sounds of low, rolling thunder became distinguishable from the crashing waves on the shore. As the leviathan drew near, lighting flashed in the distance. The speed of the leviathan didn't compare to that of the impending storm.

The sea monster reached the shore and splashed its hulking front half onto land while its back half remained submerged. It had two mammoth pectoral fins to support its weight. At sea level, two smaller fins trod water into powerful whirlpools that spun away from the beast's body. Owen imagined small fishing boats sinking from the strong undertow those whirlpools created.

Cedric climbed the fins and positioned himself on the creatures back. Owen followed and sat behind him. The water made its back slimy, but he found a secure spot to cling fast. Yara took a seat behind Owen.

Follum ran his hand down the creature's neck. "We have to part company now. I have aided you in your quest all I can." He spoke strange words to the beast. It lumbered back into the sea. Here, even with its passengers, its motion was smooth and effortless.

*He's aided us all he can? I doubt it. Someone as wise as Follum can always help.*

More lighting lit the western sky, and the rumble of thunder stirred nausea in the pit of Owen's stomach. The front edge of the dark clouds already covered the Inferno. It didn't matter how fast the leviathan could swim, the storm would reach the island first.

The smooth water ruffled into small wakes before large waves with whitecaps came crashing into the leviathan.

Owen's legs became wet and slippery. He had trouble holding onto the creature. A strong gust of wind slapped him in the face, and he skidded. His grip tightened on the scales, barely preventing himself from dropping into the water.

Ahead the storm covered the island. Owen had never seen anything like it. The blackness of the clouds absorbed all light. The water below them spun and churned in mimic of the clouds above.

A huge wave reared before the leviathan. The beast tried to swim around the wave but not fast enough. The sea creature rose with the swell and sank in the subsequent trough. Another wave mounted and crashed on top of them.

Owen slid off the creature and was submerged in the water. He spun and churned from the storm as well as the leviathan's fins. The darkness furthered his disorientation. Blood pounded in his temples, and his chest burned for a breath of air. Owen kicked, frantic to find the surface and hoping he swam the right direction. His will started to give out, his burning breath escaping when his face broke through the water. Rain beat on his head, making it difficult to believe he could safely breathe. The first breaths rushed in and put out the fire ablaze in his chest.

The leviathan circled around to regain him. When it rubbed past, he tried to snatch it, but his hands slipped on the slick scales. His head bobbed, and salty water filled his mouth. He grabbed the rear set of fins and used them to pull himself out of the water.

His eyes and nose burned and stung from the salt water. He spat in an attempt to get the taste out of his mouth, but the wind caused a constant spray, making his efforts futile.

A swell made the leviathan's tail rise out of the water. Owen's heart raced as he looked down into the turbulent water. He tried to hold on, but the tighter he griped the reptile, the more he felt like he would fall.

Through the pitch black sky, Owen could barely see Yara and Cedric. Cedric appeared to be turned around and shouting at him, but he couldn't hear words over the roar of the storm and sea. Water splashed in his ears, making hearing more difficult. He tried to shake it out, but he couldn't let go to dry them.

Yara held out her hand just short of his.

Owen stretched for her. *I can't reach that far*. The scales below her hand dried. *Of course! Magic*.

Owen held out his hand and dried the scales before him. His skin grew hot from the magic. Rain drops evaporated when they touched his hands, making his palms dry, as well. Doing this, he progressed up the back of the leviathan until he positioned himself just behind Yara.

A bolt of lightning struck not far to their left, followed by a loud clap of thunder that almost made Owen lose his grip again. *What if we get struck by lightning?* He could only hold on and hope for the best.

Thankfully they soon reached land, and the leviathan pulled half its body out of the water so they could disembark. The huge creature hurried back into the water, submerged, and swam away.

On the island, a river of lava flowed from each towering volcano. Steam rose. Torrents of rain beat down. Lava streams ran together before flowing into the sea. Huge clouds of mist emerged as the waves crashed into the molten rock.

The sky lightened to pale blue before darkening to yellow and green. From the clouds, two tornadoes reached down and dipped into the sea. They bobbed and weaved in random paths before approaching land.

Owen's gaze darted around, searching for a place of refuge, and he spotted a narrow cave near the junction of the lava rivers. "I think we could take shelter in there."

They sprinted to the cave. Yara, the smallest of the three, turned sideways to squeeze through the narrow opening. "This will work. It opens to a wide cave once you get through the mouth."

Cedric motioned for Owen to go next.

The tornadoes twisted toward them. They merged for a moment then split in two again.

Owen stuck his right arm in and felt the walls. Within his reach, the opening widened. Yara grabbed his hand and helped pull him the rest of the way through. He stood in a large, dark, open area.

Cedric's hand entered the cave, and Owen pulled him through. They used magic to dry their clothes, and the experienced sorcerer raised his staff. The tip glowed, showing the enormous size of the cave. The calm atmosphere inside gave a complete contrast to the turbulent winds and rain just a few feet away. Owen's heart settled into a normal rhythm as he relaxed for the first time all morning.

The damp, dark, charred-looking walls of this room towered above them, appearing to scale the entirety of the mountain. The path dropped in a steep slope. The whole island must have been formed by flowing lava.

"Why do you think the Great-Dragon hid the sword here?" Owen asked.

"This island is called the Inferno because of the volcanoes," Cedric explained. "There are only two peaks, but the island is also riddled with dozens of caverns. They have all carried lava, and some still do. The natural protection here would stop someone from just happening upon the Dragon Sword. I'm sure the Dragon Staff has equal geographic protection." He stopped and cocked his head, as if listening. Owen couldn't hear anything.

"Do we need to worry about an eruption while we're in here, Cedric?" Owen asked.

"I don't think so. I don't think lava has flowed through here for eons."

Yara ventured to the beginning of the downward slope. "It must go under the ground."

The path wound out of view. Cedric caused his staff to flash brighter. This time, not only the end glowed but the entire staff. With the bright flare, they could see more of the path. As it wound deeper into the ground, it split in two before it disappeared out of sight. One way had only a smooth wall around it. The other had a natural rock formation in the shape of an animal. Long powerful hind legs bent and supported the weight of a muscular-looking body. Front legs pawed at the air. A head-shaped rock in a thrown back position with a long mane gave this geographic anomaly the definitive appearance of a healthy steed. Cedric returned the light to its normal illumination.

"It's the cave from the riddle," Owen said.

He turned to Yara and Cedric, and a black creature, larger than Owen's hand, dropped from the ceiling toward Yara's head.

# CHAPTER ELEVEN

# Separate Paths

Without thinking, Owen drew his sword and slashed it above Yara's head. She looked at him as if he had just tried to kill her before she saw the two halves of the creature on the ground. Eight hairy, black legs twitched as the massive spider lay dying.

"If creatures like that live here," Cedric said, "lava hasn't traveled these tunnels for quite some time." He raised his staff again and lit it. This time, instead of a flash of light, he held the glow. From a large fissure in the sloped ceiling, dozens of hairy legs pawed and clambered to pull their bodies free from the crevice.

Two spiders fell to the floor and scurried toward them. Owen decided to try his hand at magic, and two green blasts emitted from the tip of his sword. Each struck a spider. They flew backward and folded their legs about themselves.

Yara drew her bow and loosed several arrows at the spiders as they came through the gap.

"Get close to me," Cedric said.

When they did, he placed his staff on the ground and raised his hands over his head. He clasped them together and slowly pulled them apart. A green orb formed between his hands. It continued to grow as his hands separated farther. When he stretched to his limit, he clapped his hands together again. The orb exploded, splattering radiant beams of green magic to all areas of the cave. All the spiders dropped, curled their legs upon themselves, and died.

"We need to get out of here," Cedric said. "I think these spiders are drawn to the light."

They hurried down the path to the spot where it split. They stopped near the rock formation of a steed. The path it guarded looked straight and wide. The unexpected smell of fresh flowers floated on the gentle breeze blowing out the tunnel. The other path narrowed, wound, and dropped sharply. A breeze came from this tunnel as well. It smelled of death. Owen thought of rotting garbage and the dead fire hounds. He heard a solid plop on the ground and the sound of several legs scurrying toward them.

"We have to move," Owen said. "'Take not the one protected by steed,' right?"

Owen started down the path reeking of death, much to his displeasure. The slippery ground made it difficult for him to stay on his feet, but he managed by holding onto the equally slippery wall. He tried shuffling his feet, but he continued to gain speed. With another step, he slipped, fell on his back, and struggled to regain his footing.

"You don't know any magic that will make us sticky, do you, Cedric?" he asked.

"I'm afraid not. I suppose we could dry the ground, just like you dried the leviathan's back, but we'd still have the steep slope to deal with. And right now, I don't want to take my hands from the wall."

"Guys, lookout!" Yara shouted.

Owen turned his head to see three of the monster spiders scampering behind them. The lead one jumped and landed on Yara's face. She tumbled and slid, knocking Cedric to the ground. He, in turn, crashed into Owen, causing him to fall. The three of them shot, out of control, down the passage.

A blunt object slammed into Owen's back, and the wind burst from his chest. He had smashed into the stone pillar dividing the path in two. Cedric crashed into him, and the two of them went sprawling down the path to the right.

At the edge of light cast by Cedric's staff, Owen saw Yara smash into the pillar face first. The spider clinging to her face splattered. Yara tumbled out of control down the other path. The two remaining spiders followed her.

"Yara!" Owen shouted with all the breath he could manage to suck into his lungs. He sprang to his feet on the slope, determined to climb the path and follow after her. His vain effort resulted in him smashing into the cold, hard ground face first, knocking the wind from himself again, and bloodying his nose.

The tunnel before them glowed faint orange in the distance. As they continued to slide toward it, the glow grew brighter and hotter. Soon, Owen could tell the path ended, or more accurately, it disappeared. A large hole awaited them, and in the opening below passed a river of lava.

"Prepare yourself, Cedric. We're going to fall!"

Owen reached the opening and became weightless. He sailed through the air. *Do birds feel like this?* For a moment, it seemed his speed would carry him across the gap to the path on the other side, but he fell short and hit the wall. He tried to grip the edge, but his fingers slipped on the moisture.

He plummeted, wondering if he would feel the burn of the lava before he died or if it would happen too quickly. His feet hit first. His weight came down on his knees, and they snapped. Intense pain from the broken bones blurred his mind, and he couldn't think clearly enough to figure out what had happened.

The pain eased. Cedric kneeled beside him with a hand on each of Owen's knees. A stone bridge passed over the churning river of lava. An arched doorway stood on either side. One archway showed nothing but darkness. The other had a faint light glowing from within. Cedric touched Owen's nose. The steady stream of blood became a trickle and stopped.

Owen stood and looked up to the hole from which they fell. He felt lucky he only broke both legs. Searching the walls for a foothold, or some other way back up, proved futile. They looked completely smooth and completely black.

"We have to get up there," Owen said. "Yara hit that pillar face first. She could be unconscious, and two of those spiders chased after her."

"Owen, there's nothing we can do."

"We have to! We can't just leave her. They'll kill her." He swallowed hard. "They may even eat her."

Cedric put a hand on Owen's shoulder. "Her fate rests not with us."

Owen slapped the hand from his shoulder. He hadn't felt this kind of hostility toward Cedric for two days. This time it had nothing to do with magic. In fact, magic might be the answer. If they could fly up there, or teleport, they could save her.

"Cedric, can't some magicians teleport?"

"Yes, but it's dangerous. And I never learned how. For some reason, it's a skill more easily mastered by evil users of magic."

Owen's face burned hot with indignation. Sweat broke on his brow as he tried to think of some way to save Yara. He kicked a stone that lay on the path. It smashed against the cave wall and fell to the river of lava below. A small plop and a splatter of lava swallowed the stone. The heat of the room coupled with his anger made his head spin.

Owen sat before he lost balance. "I dreamed this."

"What?" Cedric asked.

"After the emmoth attack, I blacked out. I thought you took me somewhere. That night, after you healed me, I dreamed about it again. In the dreams, we stood right here. Yara was gone. I wanted to save her, but I knew I couldn't."

Cedric appeared deep in thought.

"What?" Owen said. "Cedric?"

Cedric shook his head and looked at Owen. "It could be. It almost never happens, but I've heard stories of it just the same."

"What, Cedric?"

"You could be a dreamer. A very rare form of magic; a dreamer sees the future in his or her dreams. I, too, had a dream about the future once. I dreamed of the Wizard Rebellion's attack on Innes Castle. I never had a seeing dream again. You may never have another. But this is very uncommon."

"What? Having a seeing dream?"

"No, well, yes." Cedric stumbled over his words. "Seeing is rare in and of itself. What makes your dream exceptionally rare is timing. When you got run through by the emmoth, you knew no magic. Seeing for the rare few destined to acquire the ability usually starts shortly after they start learning magic. Almost never does a person have a seeing dream *before* they've learned any magic."

Owen examined the area where they stood. The violet-colored bridge looked as out of place as a castle in the clouds. Owen rubbed his hand on the bridge. "Someone built this."

"I'd say so." Cedric said. "I'd say it…" He looked over Owen's shoulder.

"Are you all right?" Owen asked.

"I thought I saw something on the wall."

A green spot appeared on the wall behind Cedric. Owen rose to his feet and leaned over to get a better look. Another one behind Cedric became visible when he moved. *Eyes!* They disappeared.

"You did see something," Owen said.

Two more eyes appeared behind Cedric. This time, they moved. They progressed down the wall and onto the floor. Against the purple floor, a black lizard-like creature appeared with bright green eyes. Its body wiggled and twisted as it ran toward them. The lizard closed its eyes and opened its mouth, revealing a lava-orange surface inside and a sharp ridge of teeth. It leaped.

Owen drew his sword and split the creature lengthwise. Each half fell from the bridge and splashed into the lava. They burst into fireballs and fizzled.

More eyes appeared on the wall. Two more lizards sprawled on the ground between the men and the closest room. The lizards stalked toward them. They closed their eyes and opened their mouths. Owen awaited their attack, but it never came.

"Owen, behind you!"

Owen spun to see a different lizard flying at him. A surprise attack! He slashed it with his sword. He twisted around to see the other two spring at him. Another swing of the blade cut one down, but the other hit his arm. The beast's body ricocheted off Owen, its teeth barely missing him, but the force of the impact caused him to drop his sword to maintain balance. The lizard splashed in the lava, and Owen's sword clanged on the stone bridge. It made a scrapping noise as it slid toward the edge. He dove to grab it. His fingertips grazed the hilt, but couldn't grip it. The sword teetered on the edge, before tipping off the bridge. Years seemed to pass while he watched it flutter and spin toward the molten rock. It landed with a plop and a splash of lava. It glowed red before it melted and became part of the fiery river.

"My sword!"

Cedric grabbed him by the shoulders and lifted him off the ground. With the path to the door clear, they sprinted for it, their robes flailing out behind them. They reached the doorway, and Cedric waved his hand in several small circles.

A number of the animals scuttled across the bridge and jumped at the men. Just before striking, they hit an invisible barrier. They clawed and snapped at the barrier.

Owen watched with curiosity. "Shadow lizards."

"What?"

"You've never heard of shadow lizards? When I was small, kids would tell stories trying to scare one another. We'd tell about shadow lizards sneaking in at night, or living in the wardrobe, or under the bed. If they caught you, they'd carry you away. We even had poems."

He recited one in a singsong voice:

*"The creatures you most need to fear*
*Do not dine on the flesh of a deer.*
*They love to munch heads*
*Of children in beds.*
*The black shadows of lizards lurk here."*

Owen cleared his throat and said another:

*"Shadows.*
*Lizards under*
*Beds, on walls, creeping through*
*Doors, taking children in the night.*
*Watch out!"*

Owen pointed at the creatures stuck behind Cedric's magic barrier. "I imagine a shadow lizard would look something like this."

Cedric watched the lizards without turning his attention to Owen. "I can't say I'm familiar with your tales, but I guess one name is as good as another. Whatever they are, they're certainly smart. Let's leave. I don't like looking at them."

They passed through the doorway, and a faint light illuminated the room. A stone pedestal stood in the center. Above it hovered an immaculate white sword, the color of fresh fallen snow. The pommel formed the head of a dragon, and the grip looked like scales. A well-fashioned guard of dragon wings wrapped around it.

"The Dragon Sword," Owen said just louder than a whisper. Awe did not express his true feelings at seeing it.

<u>CHAPTER TWELVE</u>

# The Dragon Sword

"Guys, lookout!" Yara shouted.

Three of the spiders came down the path after them. She tried to grab her bow from her back, but the string snagged. She screamed as one of the spiders leaped. It landed on her face. Hooks at the end of its legs dug into the flesh.

Her feet slipped, and unable to see at all, she tumbled. She accelerated down the path. Human legs brushed her back, and a body fell atop her. Cedric let out a grunt, and he landed beside her. She struggled to get free of the spider.

Cedric fell away, and she almost regained her footing when she slammed face first into something. Bright light filled her vision in the dark cave. The spider smashed and fell from her. Its blood and bodily fluids burned and stung her eyes. Some fluid squirted up her nose, overwhelming her with the stench of rotting tomatoes.

She toppled backward. Her head spun from the impact. She tumbled deeper down the tunnel. The light from Cedric's staff faded the farther she fell. At the bottom of the tunnel, the ground leveled, and she skidded to a stop.

Yara hurried to her feet, unable to see much but afraid the other two spiders would spring at her any moment. A stone archway stood behind her, and an eerie, faint blue glow lit the doorway. She entered the room, hoping to see the spiders before they attacked. Torches with unnatural blue flames lit the walls. Shadows flickered in time with the flames.

One long, hairy leg probed into the doorway. Her head throbbed from the crash, but she couldn't worry about that now. She removed her bow from her back and nocked an arrow. When the creature pulled its body through the archway, she loosed the arrow. It landed home. Only the feathers protruded between the spider's eight eyes.

The second spider wasted no time trying a different attack. It jumped into the room, and instead of creeping toward her, it leaped. The flickering of the torchlight didn't help her lock onto her target. She slung an arrow at it, only to miss and have the arrow splinter on the stone wall. She nocked another arrow and took a slow, deep breath. When the spider made its final leap, she released the arrow. It sailed through the beast, and Yara could see a blue torch flickering through the hole. She stepped aside, and the dead spider sprawled on the floor.

If Owen and Cedric had followed her path, they would have reached her by now. They must have taken a different path. She didn't know why. Perhaps the path split, and they couldn't control their descent enough to follow her.

She examined the room. The dark doorway in front of her led back to the tunnel. Behind her stood an identical doorway, but the room on the other side shown with a faint white light.

Since she couldn't go back the way she came, she headed for the door to the lit room. As she walked, her shadow bounced and danced from the flickering blue torches: torches that could only exist with magic.

Just before she reached the door, her shadow stopped moving. The peculiarity of this caught her attention. She stopped and watched it. Her shadow appeared to pop out of the ground. Instead of lying flat, it took up a definite space. The shadow pulled itself onto its elbows, knelt, rose to its feet.

It had the exact silhouette of Yara. It just lacked any definition or color. It walked to the doorway, turned to Yara, and said in her own voice, "You must defeat me, if you wish access to the treasure which I defend."

She didn't know what to do. The shadow stood unmoving, facing her. She took a step toward it, and the shadow drew a shadow-bow and a shadow-arrow. She chanced another step, and the shadow figure released the arrow.

Yara executed a back handspring, and the arrow passed below her as she glided through the air. She felt the wind from its feathers as it passed. Her heart pounded through her chest and all the way up her throat. Her pulse throbbed at her temples.

Landing on her feet, she steadied her breathing. She removed her bow and slung an arrow at the shadow in one motion. The arrow struck the shadow square in the chest but passed through without the figure so much as flinching.

Yara stepped forward, and it raised an arrow. Not sure if she could dodge another, she took a step backward. The shadow lowered the arrow.

*So, it doesn't want to fight me. I must figure out how to defeat it like a puzzle. My arrows don't affect it, and I don't want to take a chance with its arrows striking me.*

Yara looked around the room for a clue. Strange shadows continued to jump in and out of all the crevices. The moving shadows disoriented her senses, but one shadow didn't flicker. The one she had to pass stood as solid as another person in the room.

"Thank you for teaching me magic, Cedric," she mumbled to herself. As an afterthought she added, "Wherever you are."

She nocked an arrow, but this time, she used magic to make the tip glow bright white. She released it, and when it reached the shadow, it stuck in the center of its chest. The light radiated outward, and the shadow disappeared from the point of impact out to its extremities.

The arrow fell to the ground with a clunk, and shadows from the corners of the room flew and landed in a blob in the center of the floor. The shadow mass stretched out and slithered like a snake toward Yara. She tried to step away, but it moved too quickly and with too much agility. When it met her feet, it spread out and reformed as her own shadow. The torches flickered, and her shadow danced across the ground again.

She walked toward the room, waiting for another figure to appear, but none did. When she entered the room, she saw a sword, whiter than anything she had seen before.

From across the room, she heard Owen's mesmerized voice say, "The Dragon Sword."

* * * *

Owen rushed to the Dragon Sword, reaching for it with his outstretched right hand.

"Owen, wait," Cedric said. "Remember the riddle. 'Second into the fire maze should seize the sword or feel the blaze.'"

Owen paused for just a second. "I did enter the cave second. Yara entered first, I went second, you came in last."

Cedric began too late, "That's not the only—"

Owen grasped the hilt and jerked his hand away from the burning heat in an instant. He fell to his knees, clinching his smoldering hand with the uninjured one. He couldn't imagine his hand hurting worse if he had dipped it in the river of lava. He tried to scream, wanted to scream, *needed* to scream, but the pain sucked the breath from him. His fingertips turned black. He watched in horror as the blackness crept toward his palm.

Cedric ran to him. Owen took a double take as he spotted Yara running next to Cedric. Owen reached for Cedric's staff with his left hand.

"Let me heal it," Owen gasped.

He held the staff to his charred right hand and focused on healing, but the painful darkness continued to spread.

Giving up, he handed the staff back to Cedric. "All right, you heal it."

Cedric gently took his hand and lifted it toward his face to examine it in the light. "I'm afraid I can't. Traditional magic can only heal physical wounds created by solid objects. Potions can heal both magical and physical wounds. Non-traditional magic created this wound. If it can be healed, which I doubt, it will take a special potion."

Blackness covered every part of Owen's hand where it had touched the sword. The searing pain continued.

"I don't understand," Owen said. "I entered the cave second."

"Riddles don't always have such obvious, literal meanings," Cedric said. "It doesn't matter that Yara entered the cave before you, or if a hundred other people had already entered the cave. All that matters is the person trying to claim the sword."

Even through the pain, Owen started to understand. "So the 'second into the fire maze' must refer to a part of me." He looked at the burnt right hand.

"Exactly," Cedric said. "Think of how you passed through the entrance. You should have claimed the sword with your left hand, the second to enter the fire maze."

Owen stood. His right hand, along with burning agony, felt like it weighed twice what it should. He grabbed the Dragon Sword with his left hand—his second hand to enter the cave.

As he took it off the pedestal, a mist covered the ground. The temperature dropped, and the mysterious light dimmed. The mist rose to the ceiling and formed into the enormous shape of a dragon.

The mystic glow of the Great-Dragon's spirit lit the cave. Owen took a step toward it. The spirit seemed like a solid object in the room with them, yet he could see the cave wall through the misty body.

"I am the Great-Dragon," said a booming voice. "Who has earned the right to wield the Dragon Sword?"

Standing tall and speaking boldly, Owen said, "I am Owen, from the Central Domain."

"Why do you seek the Dragon Sword, Owen? Power? Wealth?"

"No. I require a dragon's aid to complete my quest. A magician told me if I found the Dragon Sword, a spell would lift, and I could ride a dragon to Ice Island."

"You speak true. As long as you have possession of the Dragon Sword, you can see dragons. However seeing a dragon differs from having the trust of a dragon, and without trust, you cannot ride a dragon."

Owen's chest swelled with confidence. He had inherited his father's ability to gain people's trust... *But a dragon's not a person.* "How do I earn a dragon's trust?"

"You must have a pure heart. Anyone seeking personal gain would find an end to their journey here."

The Great-Dragon stared at Owen. Its white eyes could have been glass or stone. A tiny black spot moved and scanned him. He felt its gaze sinking into him. He knew the dragon examined his character. And he had no doubt the Great-Dragon, even as a spirit, could put an end to anyone with bad intentions. His arm and neck skin crawled as the spirit continued its examination. A pang of guilt struck him when he remembered the dragon-mail armor. *Will the Great-Dragon sense this? Will he stop our quest or take my life?*

He jumped when the Great-Dragon spoke again. "You may ride a dragon, Owen, but you first need to understand the nature of dragons."

Owen sheathed the Dragon Sword. It fit perfectly into the scabbard from his lost sword.

"Dragons are not pets," explained the Great-Dragon, "and they cannot be tamed in the same manner a wild cat or dog can. They will listen to you if you possess one of the Dragon Relics. They will understand you well, but they lack the ability to communicate as well as I can.

"Magic makes them invisible. Only someone bearing one of the two relics can see them. This protects the dragons from hunters. But if the person in possession of a Dragon Relic touches a dragon, the penetration of the magical barrier will make the dragon visible to all humans—for the duration of the contact."

The mist dragon stared at Owen with all the intensity of any solid creature. "As possessor of a relic, you may call upon a dragon close enough to hear your voice. But when you finish with the dragon, you *must* release it from your services. Failure to do so will result in the dragon's temper becoming erratic and dangerous.

"Finding a dragon can present a challenge. They prefer warmer climates. Most dragons live in the far western portions of Wittatun, near the Inferno and Death Desert. Some do prefer to spawn in cooler climates, but a new mother dragon will likely not assist you."

Owen turned his attention to his companions. "It's a good thing dragons like the Inferno. We'll need their help just to get off this island. Our ride swam away, remember?"

Cedric stepped forward. "Great-Dragon, can you help us to the surface so we don't have to traverse this cavern again?"

"Of course," the Great-Dragon said.

Owen felt his skin grow numb. Even the throbbing in his hand faded. He felt weightless, and the three of them rose from the ground. The cave wall appeared through Cedric and Yara's transparent bodies. Owen assumed he, too, must be transparent, but he didn't want to see his body as a wisp of smoke.

They rose to the ceiling and passed through without feeling a thing. Soon, they stood in the large room where they had entered the cave. Owen remembered the spiders, and his gaze darted around the room.

"As possessor of the relic this cave guarded, you no longer need to fear the magical beasts created to protect it." The Great-Dragon's voice echoed off the stone walls.

"Thank you, Great-Dragon," Owen said. "What about my hand? I used the wrong hand to remove the Dragon Sword from its pedestal. Can you heal this burn?"

"No. Argnam created that curse to protect the relics. The Dragon Staff contains a curse of its own. The Dragon Sword belongs to you as long as you live, Owen. When your life comes to an end, the magic used at its making will bring it back to its resting spot in this cave."

A thicker mist than the dragon formed at its feet and rose to cover the great beast. When the mist dissipated, so went the Great-Dragon.

# CHAPTER THIRTEEN

# The Ruins of Ice Island

The raging storm that had chased them into the cave had not relinquished. Heavy rains obscured Owen's vision of the mainland of Wittatun as he peered through the crevice of the cave east toward Death Desert.

Cedric peered out, stepped back, and wiped rain splatter from his face. "We'll have to go out there to find a dragon."

Owen stepped to the entrance and searched the sky. "I think I can see one up in the clouds."

Yara's hand touched his back as she gazed over his shoulder. "We'll have to take your word for it. Cedric and I won't be able to see the dragon until you touch it."

Owen slid through the cave's tiny opening the same way he had come in. His throbbing, scorched hand brushed against the rock, shooting a sharp twinge up his arm. To think he could have avoided the pain with a little patience.

Outside, he walked to an open area, cupped his hands around his mouth, and shouted, "Dragon, please come down!" He had no idea if that was how to command a dragon or not, or if the dragon could hear him from such distance and through the storm. "We need your help!"

The dragon swooped to the ground and landed next to him. The ground shook as the massive reptile, not quite the size of the Great-Dragon's spirit, made contact. It folded two black wings over a ridge of brown spikes running the length of its back. Its green scales glimmered with reflecting light, even in the darkness of the storm. Two columns of purple spots marred the otherwise uniform green scales. One column ran down either side of the dragon, from the base of its neck to the beginning of its tail. Long thin scales encircled its head like a mane. Its gold eyes were two large islands in the green sea of the dragon's face.

Owen hesitated, then reached out and touched its neck. "Can you two see it now?"

Cedric had just wriggled from the hollow. "Yes."

"Let's go to Ice Island," Yara said.

Owen looked the dragon in its golden eyes. "Will you take us to Ice Island?"

The dragon bent down to let the voyagers climbed onto its back. "Ice." Its rough voice reminded Owen of the sound of cracking stones in the quarry.

The dragon flapped its enormous wings. The air around them made a whooshing sound when the wings cut through it. The rain stung Owen's exposed skin as they ascended and started soaring north-east.

Not long after leaving the Inferno, the storms dissipated and the rain stopped. A chilling breeze blew into his face. Although the air was refreshing compared to the heat of the last two days in Death Desert, the Land of Fire, and the Inferno, it made Owen cold in his rain-soaked cloths. They each used magic to dry their clothing. Owen held his charred hand into the cool breeze. The chilly air lessened the pain.

Far below them, the ocean appeared motionless. Owen started to wonder how long the flight from the Inferno to the Northern Domain would take when he saw several small islands zoom past. This made him realize the tremendous speed at which they traveled.

The continent of Wittatun came into view. They flew over it as it curved northward. Barren land stretched to the horizon. *This must be the northern part of Death Desert.* A tremendous canyon cut through the red ground. *I wonder if that's where the Great-Dragon's sacrifice happened.* The land curved southeast, and they flew over desolate ocean again.

The sun set, and the evening air grew colder. Owen couldn't believe how much the cloak Follum gave him regulated the temperature. It had allowed air to flow in and cool him while the heat of the Land of Fire pummeled down, and now it engulfed him like a blanket of warmth. He turned, expecting to see Yara shivering in the night air, but she used magic to keep herself warm.

The clear sky, the luster of the full moon, and its subsequent reflection off the ocean disoriented Owen, giving the appearance of early morning, yet with a tranquil, purple, evening sky. Large chunks of ice floated in the ocean. The ice moved past with the speed of the islands they saw earlier.

With the aid of the moonlight, Owen saw a faint ripple on the horizon that grew as they neared. Soon, mountains tore through the night sky. Their icy peaks, reflecting the moonlight, appeared to have lanterns for tops.

"Is that Ice Island?" Owen had to shout over the wind for Cedric and Yara to hear him.

Neither of them answered before the dragon said, "Ice."

"I believe that answers your question, Owen," Yara shouted in return.

As they reached the frozen tundra of Ice Island, they had to fly around and over mountains. Brown blemishes on the pure white snow became villages as they soared overhead.

"Take us lower!" Owen shouted. "I've never seen this part of the island before. I've only visited Deadlock Castle."

The dragon swooped toward the ground, but Owen's stomach seemed to stay in the clouds. Just when he thought they would crash, the dragon pulled up, and they soared just over the icy surface.

They approached the first village, and he could tell something was askew. With a temperature well below freezing, no smoke rose from the chimneys. Not a single candle burned in a window. The houses themselves pointed at strange angles. The village appeared completely desolate.

Disappointment washed over Owen. "This must be a ghost town. Let's go to the next one."

The dragon ascended and flew to another village. This one looked no better than the last: completely void of life.

A strange mixture of fear and panic started to swell in Owen. "We need to land here, Dragon."

Once on the ground, Owen's stomach lurched from what he saw. Frozen bodies, some whole, but mostly in pieces, lay partially buried with snow. Arms and legs scattered the terrain. The grand gates opening to the city had a head mounted to each of the two long spikes.

"I don't know what took place here," Owen said, "but I think it happened quite a while ago."

"Yes, it does appear that way," Yara said. "Look how much snow has covered them."

"Queen Andrea should have known about this before she left for the Central Domain," Cedric said. "She didn't say anything, though, did she?"

Owen shook his head as he examined a body. "No. She mentioned some altercation with renegade magicians, but it sounded minor. If she had known about this, she never would have left her land. She must not have known. But *how*? How could she *not* have known about an attack this large?"

"I refuse to believe the destruction of two villages in the Northern Domain could have happened without her knowing," Cedric insisted.

Owen returned to the dragon. "Let's see what else we can find. There has to be a reason."

They flew to another village, only to discover the same destruction. Forgetting about the Dragon's Breath, they headed to Deadlock Castle. It rested in a valley surrounded by mountains. The dragon circled the mountains before approaching. The battlements atop one tower had fallen, and a pile of rubble lay where another tower should have stood. The nearby village looked worse than those they saw when first reaching Ice Island. Most of the houses had burned.

The dragon angled up to find a place to land, and an orange flash of magic flew past. It hit a nearby mountain and caused an avalanche.

Owen gripped the dragon tighter. "Quick, land behind those hills."

The dragon landed, and its passengers dismounted.

Owen drew the Dragon Sword and peered around a boulder. He barely noticed the pain in his singed hand. "What do you think that was? Someone hunting a dragon?"

Yara drew her bow and nocked an arrow. "I think it's probably the person responsible for all this destruction."

Owen returned to the dragon. "Wait for us here. I know it's cold, but we have to find whoever cast magic at us."

The small hills managed to conceal a dragon. They eased around a mound overlooking the clearing leading to Deadlock Castle. Not seeing anyone, they ventured into the open terrain of a frozen lake. As the ice creaked under their feet, another spell sailed toward them.

Dodging the assault, Cedric chanced a spell of his own. A colorful burst sailed toward the castle ruins from where the attack had come. The burst shattered the fallen tower even more.

Owen took another step, and a flash of magic flew at him. This one came from the hills behind them. He dove aside and returned a jet of his own. His hex, much weaker than that of Cedric's, hit a snow-capped mountain. It only caused a small mound of snow to break free and tumble down the mountain.

Owen awaited another attack but none came. "Do you think I hit him?"

"I doubt it," Cedric said. "He's probably positioning for his next strike."

Yara searched the hills with her bow drawn. "I wish he'd hurry. We need to move. This frozen lake is too vulnerable a position. How many wizards do you think there are?"

Cedric sat up and pointed his staff at a nearby hill. A green burst of light flew from the staff, and the hill exploded. He turned, pointed his staff at another hill and exploded this one too.

"Just one," Cedric said. "He can teleport. I sense a change when he shifts."

Two balls of magic flew toward them, one yellow, and one red. "Look out!" Owen shouted.

Cedric dove behind a hill. The yellow burst smashed into it, causing several boulders to fall on top of him. The red surge hit the ground near the other two. A hole appeared where the magic landed. Melting ice radiated outward, cracking. Owen ran as fast as he could, but the weakened ice gave way. He slipped into the freezing water, spying Yara fall just before his head went under.

Icy fingers wriggled up his legs and into his chest. The pain from the intense cold paralyzed him. The world turned from light blue to dark blue, on its way to black. The excessive cold filled his mind with a stream of delirious thoughts. *I'm going to freeze to death. What a way to go. I wonder if anyone will get a potion for Father. Yara sure looked pretty at my party.* Ice water filled his lungs, burning his insides. Just before he lost consciousness, a hand reached into the lake and pulled him from the abyss of his thoughts.

The world briefly regained focus before growing black again. A dark figure stood over Owen. "I'm going to warm you up. Then you're going to tell me what in the name of Deadlock Castle you're doing here."

CHAPTER FOURTEEN

# Fissure of Tolek

The world consisted of kaleidoscopic shades of blue and white, mixed with occasional bursts of violet, red, and yellow. Owen didn't even feel the cold as he lay in shock on the shore of the frozen lake. Only as he warmed did he first notice the absolute pain of intense cold. Warmer still, the pain subsided, but the cold inside remained. Soon, warmth like a dozen heated hands slithered across his body. His mind regained the ability to reason.

Owen turned his head. On one side Yara, soaked and coughing, propped herself on her elbows. On the other he could see part of Cedric's cloak protruding from under rubble. Hot fury rushed over him, and rage boiled within. He wanted to kill the evil sorcerer, but he knew he could not win against such powerful magic, especially not in his current weakened state.

Owen found it even more difficult to speak than he expected. "Cedric. You killed Cedric."

"Did you say Cedric?" The magician looked as surprised as he sounded. He pointed his staff at the boulders, and they rose from the limp body. The man rolled Cedric over and wiped blood from his face.

Owen clambered to the foot of the hill where his mentor lay. Surprising Owen, Cedric blinked his eyes.

The new magician helped Cedric into a sitting position. "I'm sorry, Cedric. I didn't recognize you." He pulled the hood of his cloak off his head, revealing a face covered with scrapes and bruises. At least a week's worth of gray and white beard growth covered his rigid jaw. He looked to be about Cedric's age.

Cedric's eyes widened. "Hagen? What happened here?"

Owen recognized the name from Cedric's stories of the Wizard Rebellion. He must have been on Cedric's side back then based on his smile.

Cedric tried to rise. Owen and Yara reached down to help him to his feet. The older man stood, stumbled, and regained his balance.

Hagen shook his head. "I came here looking for herbs. The Northern Domain produces little vegetation, but what does grow here doesn't grow in warmer climates. When I arrived, I found a lot more than herbs requiring my attention."

"Tell us everything," Cedric said.

\* \* \* \*

White planes erupted into mountainous canyons heading north on Ice Island. The black horse looked almost blue in contrast to the pure white snow. After more than a day cooped up in a stall below the deck of a traders ship, he didn't seem to want to slow from a dead run in the freedom of open space. His rider held tight and let the horse stretch his legs.

Hagen pulled back on the reins. "Easy, Cheveyo." The horse reluctantly slowed to a trot. "We have more than three leagues to Deadlock Castle. No need to burn all your energy now."

Far to the north loomed the massive Azur Glacier. Many early settlers, upon discovering how radiant beams of sunlight reflected from the glacier, thought it an ancient communication beacon to the gods. Hagen wondered, not for the first time, why he didn't spend more time in the Northern Domain. He also knew the beauty of Azur Glacier from this distance didn't compare to what he would see up close.

The glacier tore through Loman Valley, eroding all natural landmarks and replacing them with occasional dropstones. Hagen desired to travel the smooth path north of Azur Glacier that led to the front gates of Deadlock Castle, but ease of travel wasn't his top concern. He most wanted to see the Fissure of Tolek, which split the glacier in half and created a passageway from the rough proglacial area to the smooth terminus. It displayed beautiful hues of blue, which gave the glacier its name. Such radiant colors could not be matched by the most elaborate flower garden or ornate palace.

A wind blew through the Fissure of Tolek. Snow and ice stung Hagen's exposed skin. He pulled his fur cloak tighter. Cheveyo stamped his hoofs, and for a while, Hagen could not get the horse to enter the fissure.

"What's wrong? You've been here before. Has it been too long?"

Finally, the horse relented and entered the white and blue passage. The glacial walls towered far overhead. Hagen couldn't make out the clouds through the glare of the sun reflecting off the snow and ice. When they reached the twin drumlins that marked the halfway point of the fissure, Cheveyo started prancing and circling.

Hagen dismounted. "I sense it now as well. You stay here. I'll scout ahead."

Hagen teleported to the top of the glacial wall. He didn't see anyone so he teleported past a nearby bend in the fissure. To his horror, a troll, thrice as tall as a grown man, lumbered southward. On its back, in a makeshift leather saddle, rode two people: a woman and a much younger man. He knew Queen Andrea and her son, Weylin, would not ride a troll, so he crept closer, trying to get a view of who they were. Hagen hoped the luminosity of the sun on the ice would blind them from seeing him.

He thought he recognized the woman for an instant, but he must have made a mistake. She died almost three years ago. Hagen tried to get a better view when the troll grabbed a sapphire-colored chunk of ice, roughly the size of Cheveyo, and hurled it at Hagen. The magician teleported just before the frozen boulder crushed him.

Hagen returned to Cheveyo. Knowing he couldn't run, he touched the glacier wall and melted a cave large enough to hide the horse.

He lightly swatted the horse in the haunch to get him moving. "You hide in here. We've got trouble."

Hagen magically created an illusion to make the glacier wall appear solid, thereby hiding Cheveyo from view. He turned and drove the end of his staff into the opposite wall of the glacier. The staff glowed red, and he traced a large circle in the ice. A boulder tumbled into the path. Hagen hid behind it and waited.

The ice quaked as the troll sprinted near. Fear washed over Hagen. The artifice of the ice boulder would not hide him from a skilled magician.

"Behind the ice," the woman shouted.

Hagen took the only chance he could foresee. He dove from behind the boulder and blasted two magical bursts at the troll. One missed entirely. The other struck the leather strap holding the young man. The leather split, and the young man fell to the ground.

The woman dismounted and distracted Hagen with magic of her own while the apprentice gained his footing.

"May I kill him as my Endeavor?" the boy asked.

"Aiden, you fool. Apprentices cannot request their Endeavors. I keep telling you I have your Endeavor planned. Let's you and I go and meet up with the rest of the crew. Jov can handle this one magician." She grabbed his arm, and they disappeared as she teleported them away.

Hagen already liked his improved odds. Fighting this one troll, Jov, would be easier than a sorceress, an apprentice, and a troll. He still didn't know for sure if the woman was who he suspected, but he would rather face a troll in a battle than a skilled magician.

Jov picked up the boulder and launched it at Hagen. Hagen aimed his staff true, and the ice chunk turned to cool rain. He lowered his staff, and magic erupted from the end. It hit the troll in the left leg, causing him to stumble. A black singe covered his green-gray hide. Another step and the monster lost his balance and crashed to his knees.

Hagen jumped aside to avoid the fall. He teleported behind Jov to strike a finishing blow to the back of the troll's head. He aimed his staff, and just before he ended the troll's life, a woman appeared on the edge of his vision. A torrent of magic gushed fourth. Hagen dove to avoid the attack and landed within the troll's reach.

A fist the size of a toddler struck Hagen. He flew and crashed into the glacier wall. His vision faded in and out. He saw the troll stand...darkness...the troll towering over him...darkness...a fist crashed into the glacier...darkness...snow and ice falling toward him. Just before it smothered him, the teeth of a horse clamped on his shoulder and pulled him into a hidden cave...darkness.

\* \* \* \*

Clouds passed over the full moon, making it difficult to see. Snow flurries began to fall from the night sky as Hagen finished his story. "I don't know how long I remained unconscious. When I awoke, I felt sure I had recognized the sorceress, but the bump to the head must have caused me to forget. I melted the ice, and Cheveyo carried me to Deadlock Castle as fast as he could gallop. I found the castle in the condition you see now: ruined."

"How long ago did this happen?" Owen asked.

"About a week ago, if I blacked out for less than a day—which I believe I did."

Owen scratched his chin in thought. "That's about when Queen Andrea would have left to come to the Innes Castle."

Hagen gave Owen a confused look. "Queen Andrea? She never went to Innes Castle. She's here."

# CHAPTER FIFTEEN

# The Queen's Potion

A cold gust of wind blew loose snow off a nearby cliff. It caught in the draft, and the turbulence created by the surrounding hills caused the wind to spin, forming a mini-tornado. It headed toward Deadlock Castle and disappeared in the dark of night.

Owen's mouth gaped. "What do you mean Queen Andrea's *here*? When we left Innes Castle, she remained to take care of my father."

Hagen looked startled. "I'm afraid someone else is at Innes Castle in her place. What happened to your father?"

Owen paced and ran a hand through his tangled hair. "We don't know for sure. He passed out at a banquet." *And we need to get back to him. Now.*

"I magically induced catalepsy to keep him alive," Cedric said. "He would have died had I not been so close when it happened."

Hagen rubbed the beard stubble covering his chin. "Queen Andrea didn't receive such a harsh attack. She's under some spell. Nothing life-threatening so long as I pour drink and liquefied food down her throat. But I can't stray too far from her in this condition. I need something with the healing powers of dragon's blood to revive her. I didn't know what to do, so I waited for fate to bring someone here I could send to the magician Follum to get dragon's blood. I never expected to see an actual dragon."

Yara looked as if she wanted to slap him, the way her hands were clenched into tight fists, but she held back. "You almost shot the dragon, and us, out of the sky! You could only see the dragon because Owen found the Dragon Sword!"

Hagen hung his head. "I'm sorry. I didn't even stop to think. I should have known there had to be a reason I could see the dragon. Excitement overtook me. I simply tried to stun the dragon. My magic wouldn't have killed it. But I hate to imagine what would have happened to the three of you from that height.

"I should like to have some dragon's blood on hand. A small vial would last any sorcerer a lifetime. Two or three drops will do for the most advanced potions. I've taken such a strong interest in herbs I seem to have forgotten the first lesson of potion making Follum taught me: dragon's blood has at least a dozen uses."

Yara looked puzzled. "This seems strange. Two of the most powerful leaders in Wittatun felled within days of each other."

Cedric motioned for them to follow as he headed for the castle. "We have to revive Queen Andrea. She can tell us more about what happened here before Hagen arrived."

Hagen reached in the pocket of his robe and produced a vial and a dagger. He held them out to Owen.

He stepped away from the sorcerer. "What do you expect me to do with that?"

"We need dragon blood," Hagen said. "A drop or two will do."

Owen hesitated before taking the dagger and vial. He stared at them. *How can I cut the dragon?*

Cedric stopped walking toward the castle. "Yara and Hagen, come with me to find Dragon's Breath. We need that to heal King Kendrick. We can't do anything for Queen Andrea before Owen returns with the dragon's blood, anyway."

The three of them left in search of the herb, and Owen returned to the last place he had seen the dragon. The moonlight made finding it easy, but its color had faded tremendously in the cold of Ice Island. It looked incredibly cold.

"I need some of your blood," Owen said. He thought honesty may work best, especially if he didn't want to end up broiled.

The dragon flapped its huge, leathery wings and took to the sky. It hovered far out of Owen's reach.

Owen tried to comfort the dragon, as well as himself. "I don't need a lot. Just a couple drops to make a potion."

The dragon circled with slow flaps of its wings, as if pondering Owen's request, before landing a few yards away.

Owen thanked the dragon by patting its snout. He pressed the dagger blade to one of the forelegs. The golden eyes intently watched his movements. This compounded his nervousness, so he turned his head away. Holding a deep breath, he swiped the blade across the leg. Nothing happened. He tried again with more force but got the same result. Deciding the dragon's scales provided even more protection than he anticipated, he raised the dagger over his head and brought it down with full force. The blade hit the scales and stopped. The shock of the sudden impact sent a fresh wave of pain from his scorched hand all the way to his shoulder. He may as well have tried to stab a stone.

Owen stared at the blade as if *it* had done something wrong. Then he remembered Cedric's lessons in magic. He held out the blade and concentrated on making it sharper. The edge dazzled in the moonlight. He tried to cut the dragon again. This time a slight scratch appeared on the scales, but it didn't cut deep enough to draw blood. Realizing the toughness of the dragon scales could provide plenty of protection, even for the magical blade, he put his full force behind his next slash. The blade cut about halfway through the top layer of scales, nowhere near deep enough to draw blood.

Discouraged and alone, he sat on a nearby chunk of ice to figure out what to do. A magician had given him the blade. A magician who appeared to understand dragons—at least had a basic understanding. The blade alone made no impact. A magical blade made a slight scratch. Maybe he just didn't have the magical experience to strengthen the blade enough. That had to be the reason.

He rose to go find Cedric and Hagen when the scabbard containing the Dragon Sword scraped the ice. Owen drew the sword. "I wonder." He touched the tip of the sword to the dragon's scales. Applying just the slightest pressure, the point stuck in with the ease of stabbing water. A trickle of blood ran from the wound, and Owen let some run into the jar. As soon as he removed the sword, the bleeding stopped.

"Thank you, dragon."

The dragon rested its head on the ground and let out a soft growl. It reminded Owen of a dog whimpering.

He corked the jar and set off for Deadlock Castle.

The castle looked worse up close than it did from the sky. Large sections of two walls had been destroyed. One could have allowed an emmoth to pass. The other could accommodate a dragon.

Several bodies lay strewn about. Most of them wore the armor of Deadlock Castle's army. One body in a simple chain mail armor looked about Owen's age. When he got close enough to see the face, he recognized it immediately.

"Weylin." He fell to his knees and brushed the frozen hair of the dead face with trembling hands.

"I haven't had time to clean up the carnage," Hagen said.

Owen jumped. He hadn't heard the others returning.

Hagen stood beside Owen and looked at the frozen body. "I'm sorry. I should have at least moved the body of the prince and given him a proper burial, but I've been busy trying to revive the queen."

"I was looking forward to having him as a brother," Owen said morosely. He had wished for a brother his whole life. And not just because he didn't want to inherit the kingdom. It would have been great to have a sparring partner, as well as someone to explore the kingdom with.

Cedric headed for the castle's entrance. He held clippings of a gray, leafy plant with flowers of multiple colors. "There's nothing we can do now. Let's revive the queen and see if she can tell us what happened before we return to Innes Castle."

Debris from the destroyed castle littered the floors. Banners that previously adorned the walls lay charred and in heaps. Only splinters of the doors remained.

Owen handed the dragon blood to Cedric. "I had no idea it would be so difficult to get the blood from the dragon."

"What do you mean?" Hagen asked.

Owen told them what he tried before he finally used the Dragon Sword to draw the blood. Hagen and Cedric both started laughing. Yara smiled at the men. Owen glared at them, trying to keep his anger in check.

Hagen stopped laughing. "You could have used the dagger I gave you. Dragons have a weak area where their legs meet their body. They don't have scales in that area, only leathery skin."

"Now you tell me."

Cedric and Hagen worked on the potions to revive Queen Andrea and King Kendrick. Owen couldn't get his mind to focus on such a precision-oriented task. Not after seeing all the dead bodies. This exemplified why he had no desire to inherit the throne.

He imagined the course of events during the attack. The queen ordering the soldiers to fight. How she would have retreated to her inner chamber, while the others fought and died to save her. *What was it worth?* They failed, the castle was overthrown, and the queen brought to the edge of death.

At least those fighting would have a chance to make a difference. They didn't have to be sheltered while others fought. Dying in battle seemed much nobler than dying in hiding.

*What about Innes Castle?* Surely the queen's imposter had attacked by now. How did Father's Sentry fare against the sorceress, apprentice, and troll, who were likely behind the evil deeds? Edward had skill with a blade and experience as a leader, but Owen had bested him. Besides, as he'd learned over the past few days, sometimes a sword could not compete with magic.

Cedric's voice jerked Owen out of his thoughts. "We're ready."

The desolation of the queen's chamber mirrored the rest of the castle. Hagen had piled down blankets as a makeshift bed to keep the queen warm against the drafts blowing throughout the cracked walls. Her black hair looked matted and dirty. It clung to her forehead and the sides of her face.

Yara knelt, lifted Queen Andrea's head, and cradled her.

Hagen opened her mouth with one hand and poured the thick blue liquid down her throat. He stepped away from the queen's body. "Now we wait."

Yara carefully laid the queen's head on the pillows.

After a while, Queen Andrea still hadn't moved. Owen started to lose hope. Hagen didn't seem confident in his magic keeping Queen Andrea alive. Cedric said Kendrick could live for months in his present state. *If this potion doesn't work, what hope do we have of Father's potion working? If she doesn't wake and tell us whom we are up against, we will have to return to Innes Castle blind.*

Owen opened his mouth to ask how long the potion should take when Queen Andrea's fingers on her right hand twitched. The movement was so subtle he would have thought it only his imagination had Yara not pointed at the hand.

After the slight hand movement, the queen continued to lie still for a long time. Finally, she turned her head and let out a soft sigh, the sound someone may make after taking a deep breath of a fragrant bouquet. Her eyes fluttered open and darted around the room. Queen Andrea didn't seem to recognize anyone. She slammed her eyelids closed and bellowed a deep groan of pure agony. Her lungs filled with air, and this time, she released a high-pitched scream. Laying still, with her eyes closed, the room fell silent except for her rapid, shallow breathing. Tears formed in the corners of her closed eyes. "Weylin? Is he truly dead? Please tell me I dreamed that."

Hagen placed a hand on her shoulder. "I'm sorry, Queen. Your son is dead, and the castle is destroyed. Do you recognize me? I am Hagen, and I'm here with some friends from the Central Domain. You remember Cedric, I trust. And the king's son, Owen, we—"

She opened her eyes and stared wildly. "Owen! You father is in grave danger! The Wizard Rebellion has returned!"

CHAPTER SIXTEEN

# Rebellions and Veils of Disguise

In the silence that followed Queen Andrea's terrible announcement about the Wizard Rebellion returning, Owen noticed day had begun. Dull, early morning sunlight filtered by clouds crept through the cracks in the walls of Deadlock Castle. Flurries of snowflakes danced across the cold stone floor.

Owen clenched his fists and stomped to a window. He turned and glared at Cedric. "I thought you said the Rebellion was destroyed!" A deep breath stopped his temper from bursting. "You said you killed Argnam."

Fueled in part by not sleeping in over a day, his anger boiled. He fought to control the mounting rage. A little rest would help, but they didn't have time for that. Owen didn't even know if his mind could relax enough to sleep.

Cedric's voice sounded as calm and collected as ever. "I did kill Argnam. Someone else must have revived the Rebellion."

Queen Andrea tried to sit.

Yara supported her back and lifted her to her elbows. "Is this comfortable?"

"No, but it's better than lying on my back. Necrose now leads the Rebellion. The rebels aren't as numerous as before, but they bring unmatched ruthlessness. As I understand it, Argnam at least appeared to start the Rebellion with good intentions. His struggle for power came later. This new Rebellion destroyed my army, they tortured me to get the information they wanted, and still they laid the castle to waste."

Owen's anger subsided, replaced by confusion. "I thought my mother defeated Necrose."

"We never found her body," Cedric reminded him. "I didn't think she could have survived, but she must have."

Andrea looked at Owen with remorseful eyes. "I'm sorry, Owen. I told them I planned on going to your fifteenth birthday celebration. I told them…I had agreed to marry your father." She wiped tears from her eyes and repeated how sorry she was. "I've never felt anything like that before. Their torture, I mean. I thought my insides had caught fire. Maybe they did. I don't know. My skin started to boil."

Hagen picked up one of Queen Andrea's arms and examined it. "I don't think they physically hurt you, Queen. They must have used magic to make you hallucinate. That doesn't make it any less real for you, though."

Owen sat beside the queen. "Necrose came disguised as you, and she used magic to kill my father. Somehow Cedric saved him. He put him in a magical sleep. We came here to gather Dragon's Breath. Cedric and the magician Follum believe a potion made of Dragon's Breath can revive my father."

Queen Andrea tried to stand but sank back down. She clenched her left hand into a fist and relaxed it several times. "I'm weak. I can't stand, and my arm is numb."

"You may have some complications, Your Highness," Cedric said. "The longer you go without treatment, the more permanent the effects of magic spells become."

*Enough with sitting around talking!* Owen gave Cedric a pleading stare without saying anything. He didn't have to. The look on everyone's face, most especially Cedric's, showed him they understood his concern for his father. He lay unconscious under some form of magic, while another magic slowly ate away at his body. In addition, the caretaker with whom they left him was both the leader of the reformed Wizard Rebellion and his mother's murderer.

"Necrose could have killed you, and King Kendrick, on the spot," Cedric continued. "Instead she used magic with the intention of killing each of you slowly. I believe she did this for cruelty, and nothing more."

Owen needed to break the uncomfortable silence that fell on the room. "Let's stop this palaver and get back to Innes Castle."

Cedric placed a hand on Owen's shoulder, which the king's son brushed aside. "We'll return to Innes as soon as we can. First we need as much information as we can get. It's foolish to rush into battle without knowing what we're up against."

Owen saw red as his former hostility for Cedric returned. "Don't give me lessons on battle, old man!" He turned his back on everyone in the room and began pacing. After a few moments, he faced Cedric. "I'm sorry. I let my emotions get the best of me. I forgot how much you've taught me the last few days."

Cedric nodded in understanding.

Queen Andrea started coughing, laid herself down, and closed her eyes. "I'm exhausted."

"I don't imagine you'll have much strength for several days," Hagen said.

"Let's leave the queen so she can rest," Yara said. "We can make plans in a different room."

They entered the Great Hall. A large chunk of ceiling was missing. The morning sky had dulled to a light gray, and clouds blotted out the sun. The flurries became a more substantial snowfall, and a few fresh snowflakes accumulated on the pile of snow already on the floor.

Hagen placed some chairs in a circle. "Necrose always had more of a power-driven focus. I think she may have swayed Argnam's original agenda in the first place."

Cedric nodded. "Follum always thought the Rebellion would turn sinister. I agree with your assessment, though. Necrose at least hastened the process. The Rebellion consumed her, and Argnam gave her great power—second only to himself."

Yara's eyebrows contracted to form a V over the bridge of her nose. "Where could she have hidden for all these years?"

Owen had been wondering the same thing and had a pretty good guess. "The swamplands in the Southern Domain."

Cedric and Hagen both stared at him.

Cedric smiled. "Remarkable."

Hagen nodded. "I agree. How did you come by that conclusion?"

Owen shrugged. "It seems obvious to me. She had to leave the Central Domain. She wouldn't have been welcome in the Northern Domain. The Eastern Domain fears magic more than the other domains. The harsh climate of the Western Domain was out if my mother weakened her as much as Cedric claims she did. That leaves the Southern Domain, the stronghold of the original Wizard Rebellion, as well as the likely location of the Dragon Staff." He waited for one of the others to add to what he said. No one did. "Do you think she could have found the Dragon Staff?"

Cedric shook his head. "No. If she had the staff, she wouldn't have needed to dawdle with us. She could have taken over the Central Domain without much resistance."

Snow now fell at a rapid pace through the hole in the ceiling. The sky had grown a darker gray, and clouds circled as they flew past.

Owen pointed through the crevice. "We need to leave to stay ahead of this snowstorm."

Yara yawned and stretched. "Do you think we should try to sleep a little before we go into battle?"

Owen looked at the sky again. "I'm not sure waiting here would be wise. This looks like it's going to turn bad." He paused in thought. "Plus I'm worried about leaving Father under the influence of the magic any longer than we have to."

"Owen," Cedric said, "any damage the magic will do has already been done. The entire castle could crumble around him, and the protective spell on his chamber will keep him safe. So please don't let that influence your decision. But if you think now is the time to leave, I trust your leadership."

Owen rose from his chair. "I'm certain. This storm will slow us, and I'm sure Necrose has grown tired of trying to break your protective barrier. I fear what she may have done to Innes Castle and Innes Village."

The color dropped from Yara's face, and Owen wished he wouldn't have mentioned it. Yara had been devastated when her brother died. He didn't think she could handle her parents meeting the same fate.

"Your father would be proud of you," Cedric said. "You have stepped up to many new challenges on this journey. You've shown you have what it takes to rule a kingdom."

Heat rushed to his face. "I don't know. I spent some time pondering leadership when we saw the destruction here on Ice Island. All those solders died for the queen."

"Not really," Hagen said. "They died for the Kingdom, not the queen. People only obey their ruler when they believe what the ruler stands for."

Cedric stood and stretched. His back cracked. "That's why your father's armies display such loyalty."

"Likewise, it's why the original Wizard Rebellion suffered its greatest loss when many of us left after the agenda changed," Hagen said.

"I guess," Owen said.

Yara wrapped an arm around his shoulders. "You still don't believe an army would take commands from you?"

"I do think they would take orders from me." He took a deep breath and prepared to expose his greatest fear. "I just don't know if I could give the orders to send out troops when I knew some of them would die."

Yara squeezed him tighter. "I have no doubt you could give those orders. You could as long as you believed in the cause. If sending troops benefited the kingdom on the whole, you could do it."

Owen knew Yara spoke true. He didn't intend on wasting any more time discussing it. "Let's go."

Hagen made no effort to rise. "I'd like to help, but I have to stay here. Queen Andrea isn't strong enough to leave alone, and someone should bury these bodies."

"We understand," Cedric said. "Your place is here, for now. If we should fail, you'll need to assemble as many sorcerers, and men, as you can to stop the Rebellion."

Hagen shot a stern look their direction. "You mustn't fail."

As they made haste out of the castle, Cedric produced a vial of green liquid from his cloak. "We have to split this between us. It's the potion King Kendrick needs. I don't know what we'll find at the castle, but we may get separated. If so, whoever reaches the king first needs to make him swallow it." He searched for containers to fraction the potion. "Yara, will you help us at Innes Castle, or will you return to Innes Village and find your family?"

Yara didn't hesitate. "I'll help at the castle. It's what my family would want. My brother, Brahma, died to protect the kingdom. I'll do the same if I have to."

Cedric found two more containers, divided the potion, and gave one each to Owen and Yara.

Owen examined the vial. "How should Yara or I get past your magical barrier?"

Cedric smiled. "It's so simple. It may very well be the most clever magic I've ever used. You just walk through."

"What?" Owen's mouth fell open.

Cedric raised his hands and shrugged his shoulders. "The magic will only stop someone with cruel intentions. You'll pass through without even noticing the barrier."

Snow fell in sheets and obscured their visibility as they started back toward the dragon. The cold, blustering wind made breathing difficult. Owen pulled his cloak over his face, as he saw Cedric do, to block the wind. Yara kept herself warm with magic, but she appeared to be struggling to make any kind of protective shield to block the cold wind from ripping the breath from her chest. Owen raised a portion of his cloak and motioned for her to use it.

They walked up a hill and around the boulder where they left the dragon. Seeing the creature made a sick feeling mound up in Owen's stomach. Barely visible as an outline through the drape of falling snow, he could tell it wasn't well. When he got close enough to see it clearly, the dragon was as white as the blade of the Dragon Sword. Its mouth hung open. Its forked tongue hung limp and colorless. They had spent too much time at Deadlock Castle. The dragon had died from the cold!

## CHAPTER SEVENTEEN

# Into the Storm

*How could I have been so foolish?* He had noticed its color fading when he came for its blood. He should have done something at the time, but he had only concerned himself with his own problems. Now they would have to take a boat to the Central Domain and walk to Innes Castle. That would take several days. *And what about other dragons? Do they have a way of finding out about this? Maybe no other dragon will ever trust me, even though I carry the Dragon Sword.*

The dragon's body swelled as it took in a slow, deep, labored breath. Owen let out a sigh of relief. It wasn't dead!

"What's wrong?" Yara asked.

He had forgotten his companions couldn't see the dragon. "The dragon has almost frozen to death. I need to try something."

Owen placed his hands on the dragon. Even over the gusting wind, he could hear Yara gasp and Cedric groan when the dragon became visible to them. Owen's hands started to glow. The falling snow that came within the glowing orb turned to rain, wetting his hands and the dragon's sides. The drops that fell to the ground crackled as they froze to ice. The light coming off his hands passed through the spectrum of color: orange, red, blue, white. The dragon's rightful hue returned within the orb of magic, but his power was limited to restoring only a small section of scales.

The young apprentice bore down with all his mental strength and knowledge of magic. His teeth clenched, and his eyes squeezed shut in concentration. He imagined the heat of the inferno, the molten lava flowing through the channels like rivers, his sword falling in and melting before it even had a chance to sink. Sweat beaded on his forehead. A red-orange sphere encircled his hands. It slowly grew to encompass his arms, and a quarter of the dragon regained its normal coloration. The snow that entered the warmth turned to rain, and when the rain fell, it melted the snow on the ground.

But Owen couldn't continue. He fell to the ground exhausted.

Cedric helped him to his feet. "Not bad for someone so new to magic. Not bad at all. But some tasks are too great for any individual. Yara, please help us. Owen, do you have strength to try again?"

He could feel his strength returning already. Somehow the recovery from magical exhaustion differed from the physical exhaustion he experienced sparring. "I think I do."

The magician and his two apprentices spaced themselves around the dragon, placed their hands on it, and concentrated. After a few moments, Yara's magic equaled Owen's first attempt. His second attempt couldn't quite enclose his entire arms, and he felt exhaustion creeping on quicker. Cedric's entire body glowed white. When all three achieved the utmost of their magical ability, the magic did something Owen had not expected. The glowing areas started pulling toward one another, as if being tugged by an invisible force. When they met, they enveloped the dragon.

Green returned to the dragon's body. Its breathing increased, and it stood up and flapped its huge wings. It looked down at Owen, but he couldn't read the dragon's emotions. He didn't know if the dragon felt angry for them abandoning it, or grateful for the warmth.

It lowered itself, and they wasted no time climbing on its back to leave the cold of the blizzard. The great creature took to the sky. The wind wailed harder the higher they climbed.

Owen patted the dragon's neck. He had to shout to be heard over the wind. "Please take us to Innes Castle!"

The dragon turned south and rushed faster than any horse Owen had ever dreamed of riding into battle. He pulled his cloak across his face to block the painful sting as the snow pelted into his skin. Yara scooted up and pressed her face into his back. The dragon looked over its shoulder and must have realized their discomfort. It arched its back, took a huge flap of its wings, stretched its body long, and pointed straight up.

A hand of ice seemed to grab and clench Owen as they entered the cloud. He tried to breath but couldn't pull in even the slightest breath. The dragon's scales lost their luster, and gray dulled the green. When Owen thought the dragon would lose its strength and they would all plummet from the sky to their deaths, they broke through the top of the cloud. The sun shone like a beacon of welcome. Although the air still had a chill, the sun warmed them. They resumed their southern course.

The snowstorm ceased over the Northern Straits. The air warmed, and the dragon's color became a radiant green again. Owen lowered his cloak and enjoyed the breeze in his face.

The dull browns of the extreme northern part of the Central Domain soon gave way to warm greens of firs, pines, and spruces marking Vivek Forest. Rarely could they even glimpse the ground through the dense foliage. Just as the green conifers became speckled with yellows, oranges, and reds of the occasional deciduous tree, a clearing in the forest opened on a small village. Smoke rose from the chimneys, and people appeared, no larger than beetles scurrying about.

A joyful feeling built in Owen's stomach. "That must be Eliska Village! They don't appear to have been attacked. I don't know if that means the Rebellion didn't waste time attacking villages on its way from Deadlock Castle to Innes Castle, or if they just bypassed Vivek Forest."

Yara's voice came right next to Owen's ear. "I think we'll take it as a good sign, either way."

The forest closed around the clearing and for a while longer, they soared over treetops. The wood stopped as abruptly as it started, revealing fields of colorful flowers and green grass plains stretching to the horizon. A black speck grew into an ominous cloud brooding motionlessly as they approached Innes.

Owen reached over Cedric's shoulder and pointed. "Do you think that's the same storm we faced at the Inferno?"

Cedric nodded. "I'm sure of it. And it doesn't look as if it has grown any calmer."

Lightning flashed, turning the clouds white and purple. The storm appeared to be west of Innes, but their chances of arriving prior to it seemed impossible. To make matters worse, in the far south, more storm clouds loomed. A gut feeling told Owen that both storms, birthed of magic, would converge over Innes Castle.

Owen scratched the dragon's back. "If you've got any extra speed you're holding back, now would be the time to use it!"

The dragon looked over its shoulder. As if it understood the urgency of their situation, it lunged forward, almost causing the three riders to fall.

As Innes Castle drew near, the joyous feeling Owen had felt since seeing Eliska Village sank. From the distance, he could tell it hadn't received the damage of Deadlock Castle, but one of its towers had crumbled to the ground.

They had managed to beat the storm to the castle, but just barely. As the dragon slowed in its approach, the wind in Owen's ears died, only to be replaced with the rumble of thunder.

"Just fly over," Owen instructed the dragon. "Let's try to see what we're dealing with."

A shrouded figure stood at the front gate. Bodies lay in the courtyard. The dead wore the armor of the King's Sentry.

"Land in the courtyard," Owen instructed the dragon. To his companions, he said, "They expect us to come in the main entrance. Maybe this will catch them by surprise."

The dragon landed, and they climbed off. Owen's shoulders stiffened. His stomach tightened, and his palms started sweating. He had never been anxious prior to battle before. But he had never fought with death on the line, either.

Several bodies of fallen members of the King's Sentry lay strewn about the courtyard. The gusting, churning wind carried pungent whiffs of decaying flesh.

The sky looked darker than the shadow lizards in the inferno. Lightning sparkled like the brightest explosions of magic. A stampede of emmoths would make no sound over its rumble. Clouds churned as the storm from the west collided with the one from the south. Rain began to fall. A few drops sprinkled their faces. Owen looked up at the clouds, and the storm struck with all the fury of a raging ocean.

## CHAPTER EIGHTEEN

# Welcome Home

Raindrops the size of tadpoles beat down, stinging like hail. Puddles immediately formed throughout the courtyard, and mud splashed where the grass had worn thin during the tourney five days ago.

*Had five days passed? Had* only *five days passed?*

The memories of the last few days whirled through Owen's head like the winds from the storm: winning the tournament, his father falling ill, fighting fire hounds, learning magic, venturing into the inferno, finding the Dragon Sword, learning the truth about Queen Andrea, the return of the Wizard Rebellion.

Owen shook away the memory. "We have to get the potion to my father. We can worry about Necrose and the Wizard Rebellion after we've saved him."

"I suspect we will find Necrose and your father in the same location," Cedric said, "but I understand your concern. Any lingering effects Necrose's magic will impart on your father will not be altered by a few moments more. We will go to your father, but not so quickly we make ourselves more vulnerable."

Owen turned to the dragon. "You can return to the land of fire now, or you can stay and help us fight."

The dragon spread its wings. "Fi."

Owen peered into its golden eyes trying to read its thoughts. "Does that mean fire or fight?"

"Fi," the dragon repeated, and took to the sky. It flapped its enormous wings and disappeared over the western castle wall.

"I guess that answers my question."

They turned to an entrance they could cut through to get to the Keep quicker, and two wizards appeared. The instant they materialized, they each fired a spell, and two balls of light soared toward Owen, Cedric, and Yara. Owen leaped, thrusting his shoulder into Cedric before a blue blast hit the older man. The magic struck the ground, leaving a crater large enough for the two of them to fit.

Yara ducked behind a tree, and the orange magic struck it. The tree burst into flames. Yara scurried away, and Owen shielded himself from the heat. The tree crumbled to ashes, and the fire extinguished almost as quickly as it started.

Cedric raised his staff and fired two bursts of magic at the wizards. They teleported away. He sent another burst of magic at the highest wall of the castle overlooking the courtyard. One wizard reappeared just as the magic struck. The wall crumbled, and the wizard fell to the ground. His body lay still amongst the rubble.

The other wizard reappeared behind them, sending a succession of magic their way. Owen dove out of the way before the magic made a huge fire where he had stood. He heaved a sigh of relief to see Yara and Cedric had also dodged the spells. Considerable heat made him turn his head and shield his face from the flame.

Cedric huddled in close to Owen and Yara. "You two sneak around the wizard. I'll try to keep him busy enough that he doesn't notice your cloak, Owen. If he doesn't realize you know magic, he won't consider you a threat. If I can keep his attention focused on me, you can attack from behind."

Cedric stood and unleashed a barrage of magic the likes of which Owen had never seen. "Go now!"

They hurried to a position behind the wizard. The wizard held a hand toward Cedric, and what looked like a shield made of light absorbed the magic. Each strike of magic pushed the wizard backward.

Yara jumped over the swollen, rotting body of a Sentryman. When Owen tried to jump the body, his foot kicked it, sending a cloud of flies buzzing. They settled back to the flesh, apparently unaffected by the torrent of rain. The putrid smell that arose from the disturbed body made him struggle to keep down the gorge crawling from his stomach to his throat. He couldn't remember the last time he had eaten, but whatever remained in him wanted to escape with the ferocity of animals trying to flee burning woodlands.

Owen motioned for Yara to stay put while he maneuvered to a different position to divide their pending attack, making it more difficult for the wizard to defend. He got into position and signaled for her to strike.

Before she could attack, the wizard broke his defense of Cedric's magic and teleported behind Owen. Magic flew at all three of them. Owen rolled and, using the Dragon Sword as a focal point, sent a stream of fire toward the wizard. He evaded the fire attack, but a burst of magic from behind him struck the wizard in the center of his chest. He crumbled to the ground.

Cedric hurried in Yara's direction. Owen could only see a pile of rubble where his longtime friend had once stood. He sprinted to her and started casting aside the pieces of the fallen castle wall small enough to lift.

Cedric pushed a hand against Owen's chest. "Step back." He raised his hands, and as he did, the rubble lifted off Yara. She lay motionless, blood flowing from several cuts on her head, arms, and legs. The rain washed it away, revealing deep gashes.

"Is she…" Owen started, but he couldn't finish the question.

"No," Cedric said. "She's alive. The dead don't bleed like this." He put his hand on her head and wiped the blood away. When he finished, only unblemished skin remained. He moved on to her arms and legs, healing them as well.

A flash of lightning revealed a dark green spot on the pocket of Yara's tunic. Owen reached into his own pocket and felt the intact jar containing one of the now two remaining measures of the potion needed to revive his father.

Cedric looked her over. "I could make a potion to wake her, but we don't have time now. Let's move her out of the rain to a place she won't be discovered."

They carried her to an awning next to a stone archway. A large shrub concealed her from view.

Cedric covered her with some loose branches to further conceal her location. "If she revives before we stop Necrose, she can find us.

Otherwise she'll be safe here for a while, and we can come back for her when we've finished."

They headed to the outer bailey. An overwhelming stink of livestock waste greeted them. During the siege, no one would have bothered cleaning stalls. A human body donned in the armor of the King's Sentry lay in the path leading to the door into the castle. Remembering the stench created when he disturbed the last body, Owen gingerly stepped across this one. He had almost cleared it when a hand reached up and seized his ankle.

"Ma…Ma…Master Owen," the man croaked.

Owen did not recognize him under the cloak of blood. The man tried to hoist himself onto his elbows and failed. Owen helped him roll over. The dragon crest on his breastplate, silver on the Sentrymen, stood out in brilliant green: the mark of the King's Shield.

"Edward!" He used magic to heal Edward's wounds exactly as Cedric had done moments earlier for Yara. With the blood removed, color returned to the man's face.

He smacked his lips, trying to speak. "So thirsty."

Cedric held his staff over Edward's mouth. It cooled, and water dripped into the Shield's mouth.

After a few swallows, Edward stood, stumbled, and regained his balance. He looked inquisitively at Owen. "I didn't know you knew magic. No wonder you bested me in the tournament."

Owen felt the man's normal verbosity had returned. "I've only started learning." He changed the subject to the business at hand. "We have a potion for the king."

The shocked look of memory smeared over Edward's face. "The queen, Owen. Queen Andrea has gone mad. After you left, she ordered the Sentry to leave the castle in search of the king's assailant. I refused to follow the order. I told her the Sentry needed to remain at the castle to ward off another attack. She became furious and started attacking. Five magicians appeared and helped her. Many of the Sentry perished."

"That's not Queen Andrea," Owen said. "The real queen is recovering from a similar attack at Deadlock Castle. Necrose came in disguise. She has reformed the Wizard Rebellion."

The color that had returned to Edward's face drained, and he turned the dull white of parchment. Everyone at Innes Castle remembered the attack three years past. "Of course. Only the Wizard Rebellion would attack King Kendrick." A steely look of determination passed over Edward's face. "In my mind, this is your kingdom until King Kendrick revives. What are my orders, Master Owen?"

"Find as many living members of the King's Sentry as you can. You'll find a wizard in the courtyard. If he's still alive, restrain him. Keep up your guard, there may be at least three other wizards around here, as well as Necrose, and possibly a troll.

Edward left by way of the door to the courtyard through which Owen and Cedric had entered the bailey. He seemed as voracious for battle as ever.

Owen hurried to the opposite door. "Let's go through the Throne Room and take the escape passage behind the throne. It comes out near the Palace Keep."

They passed through the Great Hall. The dishes from Owen's birthday feast still littered the table. He barely noticed the smell of rotten food after the stench of death in the courtyard and feces in the bailey. For the first time, he wondered where the pages, squires, and all the castle staff had taken refuge. So far he had only seen bodies of the King's Sentry.

Entering the Throne Room, a voice boomed. "Owen! Welcome home! I've waited so long for your return."

In the king's throne sat the apprentice Owen had faced in the dueling tournament. *How dare he sit in the king's throne. How dare he sit in my* father's *throne.* He didn't know, or care, why the apprentice had waited for his return. Owen, in his rightful place as King Kendrick's son, drew the Dragon Sword and marched forward to remove the slime from his father's chair.

CHAPTER NINETEEN

# Shroud Unveiled

A look of smug satisfaction overcame the apprentice. Stringy black hair framed his face and swayed when he spoke. "Stop!" he shouted, and orange light illuminated the room.

Owen's legs stopped moving. He tried to lift them, but they remained securely fastened to the floor. He looked to Cedric for assistance, but the older man's entire body had been frozen in place. The apprentice must have immobilized Cedric's arms in an attempt to reduce the magic he could do, yet Owen's arms moved freely.

"Let's try to talk like civilized individuals," the apprentice said, walking toward his adversary. He limped with every other step. Owen did not remember him having a limp in the tournament. In fact, his agility had surprised him. "Killing you is my Endeavor, Owen. I was supposed to finish you in that silly tournament, but I had to make it look like an accident. So I held back my full capabilities, and you defeated me before I could earn my rank."

He rubbed his bad leg. "I'm pleased to see you've returned. My master, Necrose, has punished me for my shortcomings. She has permitted me a second chance should you make it back alive, and here you are."

He reached out a hand, and a staff flew to him from across the room. "I underestimated you before. I won't do it again."

Owen pointed the Dragon Sword at the apprentice. "You've already underestimated me by only paralyzing my legs." A bolt struck the young Wizard apprentice in the center of his chest. He flew back to the throne, slammed into it, and fell face first onto the ground.

The spell broke like the young man who had cast it, freeing Owen and Cedric.

Cedric smiled at Owen. "I'm starting to think you can get by without me."

Behind the throne, green and gold curtains covered an escape passage: one of many secret corridors throughout the castle enabling the king to avoid danger. They traversed their way through the dark hall, to a damp underground tunnel, and back up to a trapdoor in the floor of the armory.

They left the armory to find the storm still raging. A layer of walnut-sized hail littered the ground, and Owen hoped they had provided enough protection for Yara. They hurried through a flower garden to the Palace Keep. He slammed the door to the Keep to block the storm, only to turn and find Queen Andrea descending the spiral stairs.

She rolled her eyes. "Aiden just didn't have what it takes to be a wizard. Twice I charged him with killing you, and twice he failed. Jov, to me!"

A door crashed open to the left of the men, and Weylin slumbered through.

The queen raised her arms in the air. "I guess there's no need for disguises any longer."

What looked like water sprung from her fingertips, soaking Weylin and herself. The water washed away their façade. The queen's hair grew long and blonde as the water washed over it. Her skin became yellowish-orange, and her eyes grew as dark as a shadow lizard. The flawless left side of her face contrasted the deeply marred right side. A star-shaped scar encircled her eye.

As a small boy, Owen often played with rapid beans. When they got wet, they grew so fast he could actually sit and watch the plant grow. He remembered them seeing the water wash over Weylin. His shoulders broadened. His arms, legs, and neck grew thick, like the castle's buttresses. His head had almost reached the ceiling when the fountain stopped.

Where Queen Andrea and Weylin had stood a few moments before now stood Necrose and a towering troll. For the first time in three years, Owen stared at the woman who had murdered his mother.

Necrose spun on the stairs. "I'll leave you three to play. I have work to finish. Jov, do whatever you must to stop Owen." She hurried up the stairs that lead to the King's Chamber, leaving the two men to face the troll.

"Cedric, try to follow her. I'll handle this troll."

Cedric followed the orders without question. The troll lunged toward him. At the same time, Owen ran for the stairs. The troll forgot about Cedric and charged for the younger man.

He dodged to his left and felt a draft when the giant fist passed by his face. The blow intended for the king's son crashed into the wall, creating a hole large enough to climb through.

The Dragon Sword whistled as it sliced through the air. Owen's counterattack slashed the back of the troll's leg. A stream of blood ran from the cut.

The monster examined the wound. The shocked look that spread over its face gave the impression it had never been cut before. It took a deep breath and bellowed a series of snarls and grunts.

Its massive fist came toward Owen again. This time, he evaded the attack too slowly. The fist grazed his face and knocked him flat. His back cracked, smacking the stone floor. The cursed collar in his pocket dug into his side. Thankfully the vial of potion in the other pocket escaped unscathed. The troll raised his foot to stomp on Owen's head.

* * * *

Yara heard muffled voices through the crackling thunder and splattering rain. Arrows of pain struck her head with each heartbeat, but she forced herself to open her eyes. She lay in an archway behind a bush in the courtyard. *How did I get here? Where are Owen and Cedric?*

Small, melting remnants of hail flew to the ground when she threw aside the branches covering her. She crept around the bush to find the source of the voices. Three men gathered around a body on the ground. Yara could only make out outlines of the men in the dark, but she heard one say, "He's dead. There's nothing we can do. We have to look for others."

*It must be more members of the Wizard Rebellion.* Yara reached in her quiver and produced three arrows. Two she stuck in the ground before her while the third she nocked and took aim. She centered on the head of the center man and released. Lightning flashed, and she could see the three men did not belong to the Wizard Rebellion but to the King's Sentry. Faster than her conscious mind could think, she snatched another arrow from the ground. She channeled magic through the arrow and launched a beam at the one about to strike true in Edward's head. The magic deflected the projectile an instant before it landed.

Yara revealed herself from behind the bush. The Sentrymen on either side of Edward drew their crossbows, aimed, and fired arrows with almost the same speed she could.

With the arrow still in her hand, Yara swung it, and a beam of magic knocked the two arrows out of the air. "It's me, Yara! Owen's friend!"

Edward raised a hand. "Hold your fire! She's an ally."

Yara and the three men met in the middle of the courtyard with rain soaking their clothes and hair.

"What are you trying to do, girl, get yourself killed?" Edward asked.

Not taking kindly to his derogatory tone, Yara replied, "My arrow came closer to you than either of their arrows came to me. Have you seen Owen or Cedric?"

"Yes. A while ago. They headed for the King's Chamber."

Yara felt the pocket of her tunic. Broken glass ground in a sticky mess under her fingers. "I have to find them."

"I'm under Owen's orders to find the remaining members of the King's Sentry. There's not much *we* can do with our swords against the wizards."

Ignoring him, Yara cut across the courtyard, through the kitchen, and back out into a flower garden outside the Palace Keep. A large hole in the wall of the keep occupied the spot where the door used to be. Bricks lay strewn about the garden, and the flowers looked a disaster, not just beaten by hail, but trampled by foot. When she entered the keep, her shoes slid on blood on the floor. An ovular dent distorted some of the floorboards, and blood had pooled in it. *This is fresh blood.*

She climbed the stairs to the top floor to find the king's chamber. A massive spark of electricity lit the dark sky and shown through a stairwell window like nothing Yara had ever seen before. The storm seemed to keep getting worse, but she never heard the crash of thunder.

As she reached the highest stairs, she could hear voices arguing. She crept to the corner to sneak a look.

Cedric faced King Kendrick's room. In front of the door stood a sorceress with long blonde hair, sickly yellow skin, and a scarred face. *That* must *be Necrose.*

"You think you've seen the world," Necrose said. "You have no idea. Argnam and I traveled to lands far beyond anywhere you've gone. This measly Penta-Domain amounts to a small island in the vast ocean. Land masses so large they would make your head hurt just trying to imagine their enormity. And these continents have countries where wizards are the ruling class. Some counties have made common people into slaves. And others exist where wizards have wiped commoners out of existence."

"And you think this is a good thing, Necrose?" Cedric asked.

"Of course, Cedric. We *are* superior to them. We have evolved. Wizards have evolved."

"No! Anyone can learn magic. Argnam knew it. He taught me, and I have taught 'commoners,' as you call them."

Necrose laughed. "Nonsense. You can't mean that inexperienced apprentice girl I killed three year ago."

"Her, and others."

"What others? I've kept a close watch on you. You haven't trained anyone since her. I'm tired of this chatter. If you still won't rejoin the Rebellion, then I will finish what Argnam failed all those years ago." Necrose raised her staff and pointed it at Cedric.

## CHAPTER TWENTY

# Vow Fulfilled

The troll's foot, as long and wide as a grown man's torso, closed in on Owen's head. The callused bottom looked like a toad's skin. Small mushrooms grew between the toes.

Owen rolled away just before the foot smashed down. The floorboards splintered and dented, leaving a broken section in the shape of an oval. From a supine position, he swung at the troll again. He cut its leg deeper, and the blood pooled on the broken floor.

The beast charged Owen, who clambered off the floor and sprinted for the door. A few steps away, he knew he couldn't reach it in time, so he jumped aside. The troll lowered its shoulder to crush him into the wall. It missed and hit the door. The wall exploded. Bricks and shards of wood sprayed into the garden.

Rain poured down. The mid-morning sky, as dark as a cave, had the appearance of midnight. Lightning flashed, outlining the creature.

Owen stormed at the troll. An enormous hand clawed at him, but he dove and rolled between the troll's legs. Another swing of the Dragon Sword landed and cut the beast. The rain quickly washed the blood away in red rivulets.

Owen dashed to the far end of the garden and behind the wall of the Keep. His vision had only started to adjust to the dark, making his way treacherous. He tripped over a soldier's spear and splashed face down in the mud. His wet hair clung to his face and hung in his eyes, obscuring his sight even more. He struggled to his feet, slipped again, and regained his footing. As his eyes adjusted, he could make out the gigantic outline of the troll heading toward him.

The troll rounded the wall but searched futilely. Taking slow, elongated steps to stay quiet, Owen snuck past the troll and climbed the stairs leading to the battlements. He raised his sword, closed his eyes, and shielded his face with an arm. The emitted electricity from his sword grew so bright he could see it through his obscured eyes. The sparks must have blinded the troll as it let out a deep wail of pain.

Owen opened his eyes to see the monstrous outline clutching its eyes and staggering around aimlessly. The creature stumbled backward. Its foot caught the bottom stair, and it fell. Its head crashed into the castle wall with a sickening crack. Even over the sound of the storm, he could tell its skull had split. The beast lay still.

A voice called out, muffled by rainfall, "Owen, are you all right?" Hoping to see Cedric, he turned, but the shadowy silhouettes of Edward and two other members of the Sentry hurried toward him.

Owen greeted them. "I'm fine. How are your men?"

The dark shadows compounded the grim look on Edward's face. "Not well. Our members are few. We did come across Yara a little while ago. She came to find you and Cedric. I'm not sure how she could have missed you with all the blinding light."

The sky erupted with lighting like an exploding volcano. Owen saw a massive shape hovering in the air. Then thunder crashed and shook the ground.

Owen pointed in the direction of the mass. "What was that?"

The Sentrymen turned to see.

Edward directed their attention to a proximal spot on the ground. "That tree just fell. It looks as if there's a person in it."

Owen couldn't contain his excitement. "It didn't fall on its own. A dragon landed on it."

He ran to the dragon. It had a body in its mouth. The bloody cloak dangling between the reptile's teeth identified the dead body as a wizard. Owen touched the dragon.

Edward gasped. "What the…"

Owen showed the men his sword. "I have this relic. It's called the Dragon Sword. It enables me to see dragons. If I touch one, anybody else can see it, as well."

The dragon dropped the limp body to the ground.

Owen patted the dragon's nose. "I'm glad you decided to fight."

"Fi," the dragon replied.

"Fi," Owen repeated.

The dragon took to the air and flew away.

"I thought dragons were extinct," one of the Sentrymen said.

"So did I," agreed Edward.

"They're rare," Owen corrected them, "but not extinct, yet."

The four men turned as a window on the top floor of the Keep shattered. Glass rained. Shadows danced across the walls, interrupted by bursts of magical light.

Owen headed for the Keep. "Cedric needs my help. Keep searching for more survivors, and watch out for wizards."

Entering the Keep, Owen dried himself with magic. He had to admit he found magic more practical than he ever thought possible. As he ascended the spiral stairs, the noise of struggle grew louder from the hallway at the top. He turned the last corner to see Yara standing in the shadows with an arrow drawn, nocked, and ready to loose. He crept near so he, too, could see the battle.

Yara's well-trained hands adjusted her aim to follow the battle. Owen strained to hear her low voice when she whispered, "They move too fast. I can't get a clear shot. If I miss, I'll give myself away. I could even hit Cedric."

A deluge of rain poured in through a broken window, soaking the floor and tapestries. Cedric and Necrose seemed to throw themselves about with magic. Neither of them teleported, but only an astute eye could tell for sure. They would stop moving long enough to cast magic before launching back into their seemingly choreographed routine.

The fight progressed toward the door where Owen and Yara stood concealed. Cedric's magic exploded near Necrose's head, and he swiped at her feet with his staff. She evaded the attack but lost her balance long enough for Cedric to gain a step on her. He spun behind her and brought his staff in a swift motion toward her head. Before he could deliver the finishing blow, she regained her balance. She struck him in the chest with the rounded, blunt end of her rod. He crashed to the ground, and his staff rolled across the floor, well out of his grasp.

Cedric reached a hand into his cloak as Necrose swaggered toward him. She kept her rod trained at his head. His eyes lowered, and his cheeks sank, forming a morose grimace. He removed his hand to reveal a shattered jar dripping with green potion. He dropped it, and the potion dissipated in the pooling rain water.

Necrose laughed and pushed the shattered glass around with her foot. "Was that for the king? I could have made him a wonderful wife."

Owen burst forth from the shadows. Dragon Sword drawn, he intended to strike Necrose down where she stood.

Necrose stopped her advance toward Cedric and turned to him. She raised her rod. "You annoying pest!"

Cedric sprang from the ground, flinging himself toward Necrose. "No!"

The magic intended for Owen hit Cedric in the face. His body spun in midair and slammed into the floor. He let out the most agonizing scream Owen had ever heard. When his breath ran empty, his lungs did not fill again.

Owen didn't need to examine the flaccid body to know Cedric had died.

## CHAPTER TWENTY-ONE

# Fate of the King

Owen's hand moved without thinking. Three balls of magic flew at Necrose. From the doorway, an arrow flew at the back of Necrose's head.

She nonchalantly deflected Owen's magic with spells of her own. She waved a hand, and the arrow stopped mid-flight and fell straight down. "You fight with anger. I thought you, of all people, would know the futility of that. I'm pleased to see you have taken up the study of magic, though. Normally I would offer someone like you a chance to join the Wizard Rebellion before I killed him, but seeing as I've killed your mother, your mentor, and soon your father, something tells me you won't accept the proposal."

Yara stood half exposed from the shadows. She didn't bother drawing another arrow.

Owen felt hopeless despair at being overpowered. "Are you crazy?"

"No, I'm *tired*. I'm tired of people thinking they're better than wizards. I'm tired of people persecuting wizards for studying magic. And in the case of that scum on the ground," she gestured toward Cedric's body, "I'm tired of magicians working hand in hand with these people."

"And you think violence will change everyone's minds?"

"No, but it will get them out of my way." Without hesitation, magic spurted from her hands toward Owen.

He acted on impulse and swung the Dragon Sword. The sword deflected the magic toward Necrose, just missing her head. It shattered a stained-glass window.

Her wide eyes followed the path of the magic. "What?"

The reversal of magic must have surprised her. Without fear, Owen advanced on her.

Necrose raised her arms. An orb like a large ball of fire bloomed between her hands. She threw it at him with great force.

Again he swung the Dragon Sword, and again it repelled the magic.

"That's not possible. A sword can't deflect magic." Necrose took a step backward and stumbled over Cedric's staff. Her foot flew out from under her. She fell on her back.

Owen lunged for her. He jumped and thrust his sword. She regained composure and raised her rod toward him. Her efforts may have ended his attack, and his life, but two arrows flew from the shadows and pinned her arms to the wooden floor. The point of the Dragon Sword came to rest on Necrose's throat. He heard her gasp, awaiting his death blow. It never came.

Yara emerged and stood beside him.

Owen's body trembled with rage, but the point of the sword at her throat did not waver. "You killed my mother, my mentor, and you're responsible for the death of Yara's brother, but you *won't* kill my father. I've despised magic the past three years because of you."

Necrose rolled her eyes. "Are you going to kill me? If you are, I'd appreciate your haste in the matter, before you bore me to death with your life story."

Owen pulled the blade away from her neck and made to swing it. Instead he slid it into his scabbard. He reached into a pocket of his cloak and produced the cursed collar. It snapped as he fastened it around Necrose's neck.

When Necrose lost her magical abilities, the raging storm ceased. The clouds dispersed, and sunlight flooded into the hall.

She stretched her neck as if the collar would loosen. "I seem to remember this artifact. I made this cursed collar for Argnam, and he used it on Cedric."

Owen grabber her upper arm. "And you won't be getting out of it anytime soon. Get up."

Yara kept her drawn bow trained on Necrose as she got to her feet. Before leading her away, Owen reached into another pocket of his robe. He removed the last remaining container of the potion to revive his father and passed through the door to his father's chamber, not knowing if the barrier even remained now that Cedric had perished, supposing it abated just like Necrose's tempest. He lifted his father's head, the king's thick hair cascaded through his son's fingers, and he poured the potion down Kendrick's throat.

Assuming the potion would take time to work, Owen returned to Necrose. With Yara's help, he led her back to the Throne Room. A door in the corner opened to a small holding cell for prisoners facing trial before the king.

Owen shoved her into the room. "I think you'll be safe here for a while."

"What are you going to do with me?"

"Nothing, but my father will try you, and punish you, for your crimes against the kingdom." He locked the door, shutting out any reply.

He turned to find Yara staring at him with a blank expression. Her shoulders sank, and her eyes filled with tears. Owen pulled her close and hugged her. She sniffed. "I'm sorry about Cedric. I know how much he meant to you. He meant a lot to me, too."

*Cedric did mean a lot, didn't he? I don't think I ever stopped to realize just how much.*

A lump rose in his throat. He fought to swallow it.

They embraced until Yara stopped crying. "I need to find my parents now. I hope your father recovers well. I'll check in with you later." She gave Owen a final squeeze and left.

Owen ran to take his place at his father's side but stopped outside the door to inspect Cedric. He rolled the body onto its back and pulled away the hood. Long, graying hair fanned out on the floor. Taking one of Cedric's hands in his own, he noticed it had already started to grow cold.

Owen cradled Cedric's lifeless head in his arms. A flash like a dream popped in his mind but disappeared. "I'm sorry, Cedric. You gave yourself for me. I don't know much about honor in the world of magic, but I consider your Life Vow to my father fulfilled. I'll make sure you get the funeral of a nobleman."

King Kendrick had still not revived, so Owen sat in a chair and waited. Before long, the adventure of the past few days, as well as the exhaustion from battle, caught up with him. He fought to stay awake, but sleep consumed him.

He dreamed of leading troops into battle, riding on a dragon's back with an army marching on foot and horseback underneath. He dreamed of lands he had never visited: swamps with poisonous air and gas bubbles that would burst into flames. He dreamed of Yara. She traveled across the ocean. He dreamed of the Great-Dragon.

Owen awoke, not in the King's chamber, but in his own. The angle of the sunlight through the window showed him it was mid-afternoon. His mind raced, still dazed from the dream. He wondered if he had dreamed all the events of the past several days. He rubbed his eyes. The charred crust of his right hand felt as rough as a fire hound's tongue on his face. It assured him that everything had happened. His hand no longer hurt but the fingers had lost much of their dexterity and feeling. It looked much worse than it felt, resembling meat that had been left on an open flame too long.

He stumbled out of bed and returned to the King's Chamber. Much of the mess he found the night before had been cleaned up.

Owen peeked into his father's room to find him in bed reading. He knocked on the doorframe. "May I come in?"

Kendrick put down his tome and smiled. "It's good to see you awake again. I started to wonder if you would ever wake up. Edward came. He found me revived and you sleeping in the chair. We tried to wake you, but you wouldn't move so he carried you to your quarters. Yara came by last night and again this morning. She said she'd be back."

"How are you feeling, Father?"

"I've been better. I have a hard time getting my left leg to do what I want. I have a walking stick that belonged to my father. I think I may have to use it from now on, but I shouldn't complain. I took a nap while you saved the kingdom."

"I had a lot of help." Owen opened his mouth to tell his father about Cedric, but the words caught in his throat. His vision blurred, and his eyes felt glassy.

Kendrick said, "I know about Cedric."

Owen managed a nod before looking away. Silence filled the room and made it hard to even think. Finally, Owen's head cleared. "I locked Necrose in the holding cell. I thought she should stand trial."

"That's very strong of you, especially after all the loss she's caused you. The ability to make decisions like that will help you become a great leader."

Kendrick listened as his son told him about the destruction he, Yara, and Cedric had found on Ice Island. He informed his father of Weylin's death and of the condition of Innes Castle.

King Kendrick stared in the distance as he pondered the information Owen gave him. He returned his gaze to his son. "We have a lot of work to do. Most of the King's Sentry perished in the attack. The castle's been heavily damaged. It's going to take a lot of people to rebuild. You'll need to go to Innes Village and invite everyone you can find to the castle for a memorial feast this evening. Morale will be weakened, and we'll have to rebuild that first. The sooner we start, the better. For now, I'm going to rest. I'll see you this evening, my son."

Owen discovered much destruction in Innes Village, but it subsisted better than the villages on Ice Island. Many of the villagers shrieked with admiration at seeing him, and at receiving the news their king would live.

The sun set as Owen returned to the castle. He looked for the distress star, but it was gone. It seemed so strange to have a star disappear from the sky. Far in the distance, a huge bird soared through the air. Or was it a dragon?

# CHAPTER TWENTY-TWO

# Heir to the Throne

Owen sent a letter to Deadlock Castle informing Queen Andrea and Hagen of King Kendrick's recovery, the condition of Innes Castle, Cedric's death, and of a funeral for the fallen.

The first stars didn't come out until well after sunset with the memorial feast underway. The dining hall contained as many people as it did for the celebration of Owen's birthday, but the chatter of people talking remained low, just more than a whisper. No musicians lined the walls to play during the feast. The great table, another casualty of the battle, had been replaced by several smaller tables assembled to accommodate everyone. The tables masked all appearance of the siege that fell with their covering of food and desserts. Many of the castle servants had fled to the village during the attack, sparing their lives. Now they busily filled drinks and offered hors d'oeuvres.

Owen sat at the head of the table, and unlike at the feast for his birthday, Yara sat to his right with her family beside her. He reminisced how he had hated seeing Cedric when he entered the room that evening. Now the lack of the sorcerer's presence created an inviolable emptiness.

King Kendrick walked through the doors at the end of the hall, not to the sound of trumpeters, as typical at a banquet, but to a roar of applause from the crowd. He didn't wear his customary formal robes, and he supported most of his weight on a majestic purple walking stick. He went to the head of the table, next to Owen, and motioned for everyone to sit.

He spoke in a voice as loud and clear as ever. "People of Innes, we suffered a great attack several days ago. We lost many of our wonderful citizens. But we are a strong people. We survived! Now it is time to rebuild, and we will need everyone's help to make the Central Domain stronger than ever."

More applause filled the room.

King Kendrick seized a loaf of bread from the table. "My first step in making the Central Domain stronger is to name Owen, my son, true heir to the throne. I introduce to you, people of the Central Domain, Owen—Heir to the Throne of the Central Domain."

The hall roared with approval as the king broke the bread. Owen felt himself blush, but he didn't feel the hesitation he had once had about inheriting the kingdom. Owen stood, and the ovation grew louder. He had always feared the thought of someone giving his or her life to protect him, but he hadn't been king and Cedric had still died for him.

The newly appointed heir said the only thing he could think to say to the attendants, "Thank you."

Kendrick passed one half of bread to his left, the other to his right. "Please be seated. We have all this food before us. We should eat it."

People sat, eating, drinking, and socializing for hours. Owen had a chance to talk to Yara's family. They wanted to know about the magic he and Yara had learned. Her parents did not have the hatred for magic the younger two had had since the first attack by the Wizard Rebellion.

Before people returned to their homes, the king made a second announcement about the funerals. Eventually, the hall cleared.

After dinner, King Kendrick put his arm around Owen's shoulders. "You know, Owen, I've always intended to name you my heir. I had confidence in you. You just didn't have confidence in yourself, but I think you may have grown more in the past six days than you had in your first fifteen years."

Owen nodded. "I know magic now, but it will take more than magic to rebuild all we lost."

"Yes, that it will."

The days progressed faster than a stampeding emmoth. Owen helped clean the debris around the castle and in the village. The noise of construction filled the air from sunrise to sunset. In his free time, when he could manage some, he practiced the magic he had learned and tried to teach himself new spells. He tried to teleport but only managed to make his clothes temporarily transparent. Thankfully no one was around to see. Sometimes Yara would visit, and they would practice together.

Late in the evening, two days after the feast, Queen Andrea and Hagen arrived to attend the funerals scheduled for the next day.

Prior to the funerals, King Kendrick assured all those in attendance that he still intended to marry Queen Andrea—the *real* Queen Andrea.

The funerals were the most elaborate Owen had ever seen. Music and the noise of celebration filled the air. Few people cried. These people had died serving their country, which was something to rejoice, not mourn. At the end, he, Yara, and Hagen put on a special service for Cedric, with a magical light show for a finale. A tradition at magician's funerals, Hagen instructed them to take Cedric's body and lay it to rest at the Sepulcher by the Sea, a special burial ground for magicians and sorceresses.

After the funeral, Kendrick found Owen. He sat on a hill behind the castle, gazing at the stars. "What are you doing?" he asked his son.

"I'm trying to see hidden messages. It's not working. Cedric showed me one once, but it's gone now."

Kendrick lowered himself to a sitting position beside Owen. He placed his walking stick on the ground between them. "Your mother loved watching the stars. I never got much from it, but she could do it for hours. Just before she died, she saw something that disturbed her. She never told me what."

Owen glanced at him through the corner of his eye. "I have an idea of what she may have seen."

The two men sat, looking out into eternity. Several meteorites streaked across the sky and burned out.

Kendrick broke the silence. "We've done a lot of work these past few days, but your real task is yet to come. The King's Sentry has only five solders. You'll need to travel the land to recruit a new army.

"The day of your fifteenth birthday, I attended a briefing from Mansfield. He told me of a new ruler in a land across the western ocean. He violently took the throne from a well-loved king, and anyone in the land who opposes him he imprisons or kills. It has never been our place to interfere in the politics of such remote lands, but the world is changing."

Owen looked from the sky to his father. His dream flashed in his head. In the dream, he led a great army while flying on a dragon. Yara traveled across the ocean.

The heir looked at his father and smiled. "I know. I'll organize the biggest army this land has ever seen. No one will dare attack us."

Kendrick placed a hand on his son's shoulder. "That would be great, but as long as people are hungry for power, attacks will happen. We have to prepare ourselves." They sat in silence for a while when Kendrick said, "I hear you discarded Frederick's dragon-mail armor."

Owen, son and heir of the king, looked to see if his father intended on giving him a hard time about it. He had his story all worked out about the horrors of killing dragons, but the king just smiled and laughed.

Owen returned his gaze to the stars, and his father joined him.

# About the Author

Eric grew up in central Illinois. He now lives in northwest Iowa with his wife and two sons. He began publishing in 2008 when he started writing a quarterly column for a local newspaper. His first short story, "*Ghost Bed and Ghoul Breakfast*," a spooky children's tale about a haunted bed and breakfast, came out later the same year. He has published more than 30 nonfiction articles/columns, four short stories, and a poem. Three of his short stories have won honorable mention in the CrossTIME Annual Science Fiction contest. *Unveiling the Wizards' Shroud* won the 2014 Literary Classics Award for Best First Novel. Look for the sequel, *The Squire and the Slave Master*, Summer 2015.

\* \* \* \*

Did you enjoy *Unveiling the Wizard's Shroud*? If so, please help us spread the word about Eric Price and MuseItUp Publishing. It's as easy as:

•Recommend the book to your family and friends
•Post a review
•Tweet and Facebook about it
*Thank you*

# The Squire and the Slave Master

# Book 2

The award winning *Unveiling the Wizards' Shroud* (CLC's Best First Novel 2014) chronicled Yara, Owen, and Cedric's quest to revive King Kendrick from a dark, magical spell. After the adventure to save King Kendrick, for Yara, everyday life has grown monotonous. The dull work of learning her father's blacksmithing trade, and the pressure from her parents to decide what she plans on doing with her life, has her nerves so stressed she snaps at her father's slightest teasing.

Lucky for her, a surprise messenger from the castle brings the king's request for her to join a collaborative mission between the Central and Western Domains of Wittatun to stop a recently discovered slave operation in a land to the west. King Kendrick and Owen want her to accompany the mission as a secret weapon disguised as a squire.

She has to keep secret not only her magical abilities from any possible traitors, but also her gender. The people of the Western Domain have a superstition prohibiting girls from sailing. But a chill wind carries the distinct odor of sabotage. Can one girl survive to destroy an evil rooted much deeper than mere slavery?

*Releasing Summer 2015*

BONUS STORY

# The Best Magic

Light dazzled across the night sky and illuminated the faces in the crowd like the midday sun. Brilliant flashes of white unicorns chased by green, red, and blue dragons disappeared in the distance. A final set of explosions encompassed the periphery of the spectators before enclosing them like a dome. The show concluded in a shower of sparks, and a roar of applause erupted.

"Thank you! Thank you for attending!" Vivek shouted over the waning exuberance. "Thank you. This was a special performance. I must soon travel to distant villages, and share my gifts with those in need. Not that I don't enjoy performing these spectacular light shows as much as you enjoy watching them, but I feel the true calling of my magical ability lies in helping others. Please stay here and celebrate as long as you wish, but I must retire early tonight. I leave before daybreak tomorrow."

Eliska watched the whole show from the roof of a small dwelling. Having seen his light shows several times, they lost their sense of wonder for her. Vivek had made his reputation with them, but she knew he could do so much more. She waited for him to greet several spectators before he headed in her direction.

Eliska waved at him from the rooftop. "Uncle Vivek, I'm coming with you tomorrow." She jumped down and sprang to stand in front of him.

"Eliska, for the last time, you can't come with me. You have school, and I'm *not* taking you out of school just to accompany me on this trip."

Eliska reached in the pocket of her robe and produced a folded piece of parchment. Vivek unfolded it and read:

"I write this with great pleasure and admiration. Eliska has applied herself especially hard these past few terms, and has completed the remainder of her coursework over a month ahead of schedule. Eliska is hereby exempt from the remainder of her studies, and has graduated with highest honors."

Elder Tomas
Headmaster of Kingsley Higher Education

Vivek folded the parchment and handed it back to Eliska.

She waited for him to reply, and when he didn't, she finally asked, "Well?"

"Well what? I wonder if this lax educational system is what we will come to expect from King Matteo's rule. Oh, what will the future hold? Do your parents approve of this? Have you even asked them?"

"Of course. They think it would be," Eliska deepened her voice to imitate her father, "'A great learning experience about life outside of Kingsley.' Besides, what else am I going to do now that I'm done with school? Get a job in the bakery, or the mill, or the marina?" She wrinkled her nose with this last suggestion.

"Why not? It would be a great learning experience about life outside of school. It would teach you to earn money and help support your family."

Eliska lowered her voice. "You know as well as I do that my family is fine financially." She came from a wealthy family, but she didn't boast about it. "Please, Uncle Vivek. It would mean so much to me if you'd let me go."

Vivek reached for the door, but paused. He turned and looked at Eliska. "If it's this important to you, you may come. But I'm leaving two hours before sunrise, so don't be late."

Eliska threw her arms around him and kissed his cheek. "Thank you, Uncle." She sprinted home. She could feel the smile threatening to tear her face in two. *Finally, a chance to see the best magic.*

\* \* \* \*

The next morning, Eliska was sitting on a stone outside Vivek's two room hut when he emerged into the cool morning breeze. In a clearing to the west, four men of varying ages sat around the only campfire that still burned from the previous night's festival. Two of them were slumped over, probably passed out, but the other two drank mead from goblets and conversed.

"Fire needs air to burn," one of the men said, with heavily slurred speech. "But if space is this 'great void' you speak of, where does the sun get its air?"

"No, you don't understand," the other retorted, equally slurred. "The sun..."

Vivek shook his head and turned his attention from the men to Eliska. "Tell me why it's so important for you to go on this journey with me."

Eliska stood and grabbed her knapsack. "I want you to show me the best magic."

"What you saw last night wasn't good enough?"

"Those were nothing more than tricks with lights and fire. I want to see real magic."

Vivek gestured toward the drunkards by the fire. "I bet they thought it was magic."

Eliska barely glanced at them as she and Vivek started walking to the northwest. "The fact they remain conscious is more magic than anything you did last night."

Vivek laughed.

Although Vivek wouldn't admit it, Eliska knew he was glad she was accompanying him. She was his only niece, and one of his favorite people. They would spend hours talking about such varied topics as how people who knew magic should properly use their powers, and if life existed on other planets. Also, she had often heard him mention the lonely solitude he felt when he would take one of his journeys.

Vivek glanced at Eliska's shoes. "It's good the central part of Wittatun is mostly grassy plains, those shoes wouldn't last a day in the southern swamp or in Death Desert to the west."

"If we had to travel in those places, perhaps you could have shown me the best magic by mending my shoes."

\* \* \* \*

Three days after departing, Vivek and Eliska arrived in Holda. A rock-slide several months earlier had caused large boulders to block a tributary of the Ottowan River. The tributary supplied the water to the Holda valley. The villagers had managed to haul water from the Ottowan River, but winter was fast approaching, and carrying water would soon be impossible.

Elder Axella arranged their lodging and escorted them around the village.

Pointing out a large wooden wheel standing stationary in the dry stream bed, she said, "Here is our watermill." Many planks were rotting, and some had even fallen off. "We've known it needed repair work for some time now, but we didn't think we could readily survive without it. Of course it has been months since it worked, and we have survived just fine. Our woodsmen have felled the timbers needed to make repairs, but we have rerouted all our strong workers to the daunting task of hauling water."

She led them to the dam, and although it was in much better shape than the watermill, it too had the appearance of several years of neglect.

Eliska tried to lift the spirits of Elder Axella. "The stone levees don't look bad. Some stones have fallen, but otherwise they seem to have held up well."

Vivek nodded and turned to the Elder. "We'll need some of your strongest workers. It won't be as important to keep them hauling water now. Keep enough people on water duty to get enough to last several days to a week and a half. I could use magic to destroy the boulders, but the levees and the dam that have been unused for several months would not likely survive the impact of the water surge. Eliska and I, as well as the workers you provide me, will make repairs before I remove the boulders."

They spent a week helping the villagers fortify the levees, as well as using the opportunity to make any neglected repairs to the watermills. On the eighth day, the village was prepared for the boulder removal.

Vivek rested a hand on Eliska's shoulder as they faced the boulders. "Eliska, you came to see my best magic, and I think you will agree this is it."

Vivek raised his hands in the air. The bright sunshine became dull and shadows covered the land. A black storm cloud formed and blotted out the sunlight, giving the appearance of night. Lightning unlike any Eliska had seen before—somehow sharper, more intense—flashed and struck the largest boulder, sending a crack through it. The report of the thunderclap made Eliska's heart feel like it stopped beating in her chest, and she had to gasp for breath. The crack in the boulder widened. The sky lit with blue and white flashes of lightning from all directions. Every bolt struck only the boulders in the stream, not coming anywhere near the villagers. The boulders cracked and split from the electricity. They further crumbled under the rumble of thunder.

Hail followed the lightning. First small pieces the size of pebbles fell, but soon chunks as big as a grown man's fist pummeled the boulders. The cracks caused by the lightning and thunder expanded from the barrage of hail. The pulverized boulders became rocks no bigger than cannonballs. Even as the large hail poured on the boulders, the villagers remained unscathed.

As Eliska watched the last boulders disintegrate, her hair flew in her face as the previously still air began to blow. Soon her hair whipped and tangled as the breeze became gusts. The cloud grew a hand as five tornadoes reached for the ground! They touched down in a shroud of dust and crawled toward what remained of the boulders. The rocks rose into the air and hovered before the cyclones carried them away.

Vivek lowered his arms, the clouds dissipated, and the sun reemerged from the dark. Water rushed past and crashed into the newly reinforced dam and levees. The rush of water into the wood and stones reminded Eliska of the thunder.

Relief poured from the villagers, tears of joy fell, and some people even hugged Vivek and Eliska. Others voiced their assuaged fear through cracked voices and tears: Had the boulders not been removed before winter, they, the entire village of Holda, may have perished.

When everyone else had returned to the village, Elder Axella said, "Vivek, I know you agreed to do this for no payment, but please let me give you something as a token of our appreciation. We have a small repository of jewels and rare metals. Is there something you would take as payment? Verily, you saved us a tremendous amount of grief had winter come and the river remained blocked."

"As I stated in my letter, I do not accept payment. I only desire the hospitality of your room and board for my work."

"Very well," Elder Axella agreed, "but know that nothing you could have asked would have been too much."

Vivek bowed. "Thank you, Elder Axella."

"Yes, thank you," Eliska added.

The Elder shook and kissed their hands before returning to the village.

"What do you think?" Vivek asked, when he and Eliska were finally alone. "Was that the best magic you've ever seen?"

"Oh, it was quite impressive," she agreed. "But I didn't come here to see the best magic I've ever seen. I want to see the best magic that exists. I think you can do better."

\* \* \* \*

Vivek and Eliska spent another night in Holda before heading to their next destination. They would have to travel more than a week to Basin Hollow, and Vivek needed his rest after removing the boulders. He had made the magic look easy, but it had exhausted him.

As they traveled, Vivek said, "I've been thinking about what I did in Holda, and you're right, Eliska. It was good magic, but I can do better. The problem in Basin Hollow will require all the magical gift I have. I don't want to spoil the surprise, but if I can solve their problems, it will take the best magic.

\* \* \* \*

Nine days later, Vivek and Eliska arrived in Basin Hollow. Two centuries greeted them over a mile from town.

"Vivek, I'm elated you arrived," the older of the two guards said. "We have one hundred men patrolling the land all day and all night. We don't have more than one thousand citizens in town so it wears on us enormously."

"Has the cause of the problem been discovered and isolated?" Vivek asked.

The younger guard nodded his head. "Yes, er, sort of. After you sent your letter in response to our request, we knew the only person in town who could have summoned the creatures. A young man's father recently died trying to herd livestock across the river. But we didn't have to worry about isolating him. Several of our strongest warriors went to his cottage on the outskirts of town, only to discover the werecats had killed him."

"Werecats?" Eliska asked.

"Magical creatures," Vivek explained. "They are created when someone inexperienced with magic tries to summon the dead. Instead of summoning the intended spirits, the novice accidentally summons evil spirits from the underworld.

"Spirits from the underworld are easier to summon, as they are always trying to return to the surface. The enlightened spirits that have gone to the World of Enchantment don't wish to return to the world of the living, so it takes a skilled magician to summon them."

Eliska felt sick to her stomach. "Why do you call the spirits werecats, though?"

"Once summoned, the spirits need to inhabit a body to remain in the world of the living," Vivek said. "They can inhabit any recently perished body, but the bodies of cats seem to be the most accepting hosts to the evil spirits. The worst part is the cats, or any other kind of inhabited body for that matter, cannot be killed."

Eliska gasped. "Why?"

"The bodies have already died," Vivek said. "They can't be killed again." He turned to address the two guards. "How many werecats have you discovered?"

"We've seen at least ten," one guard answered. "We're reasonably certain we found them all."

"Yes," the other guard agreed, "if there were more than ten we would have seen them by now."

"I assume you have sick villagers," Vivek said.

The older guard grew pale before he answered. "Yes. We had a lot of fatalities when the first werecats appeared…before we knew what was happening. But since we formed the Century Patrol attacks have become rare."

"It's horrible, though," the other guard added. "Even the people who suffered only small scratches from the cats have had difficulty healing."

"They've become infected," Vivek said. "They'll need lots of rest, and their wounds must be kept clean. I don't know any magic to heal them. Eliska and I will help you care for the sick. In the meantime, I'll set traps to catch the werecats. When we have them all, I'll diminish them all together."

\* \* \* \*

The degree of sickness varied greatly. Some people started with tiny scratches on their hands and arms, which in turn caused their entire arm to swell and turn red. Other people who had been bitten lay unconscious, blue faced, and gasping for breath.

Eliska and Vivek turned a large communing hall near the center of town into a makeshift medical facility. The sick were sorted into rooms based on their varying needs. The people with minor injuries could reside at home, as long as they came for treatment every day.

The appearances of the werecats were as diverse as the wounds they caused. Some were a smaller breed of cat domesticated by the community, while most others were the pumas that flourished in the hills and mountains surrounding Basin Hollow. One werecat embodied a once dead lion. Usually rare around Basin Hollow, occasionally a pride would stray into the area when prey in the lower planes became scarce. Vivek made traps out of wood and rope, and Eliska baited them with fish and wild game innards.

Within a few days, they had captured all the werecats. Most of the sick showed signs of improvement, but a few of the more severe cases had passed into the World of Enchantment.

The elder member of the Century Patrol, whom Vivek and Eliska had met upon arrival, was named Estaron. The three became friends as the days passed.

Vivek said to Estaron, "Take some of the Patrol and gather all of the caged werecats in the valley north of town. This evening I will send them back whence they came."

That evening very few people from Basin Hollow gathered to watch the diminishing of the werecats. Death was sacred to most Wittatonians, and they did not feel comfortable attending a ceremony so closely related to the underworld.

Vivek and Eliska placed all the traps in a circle, and Vivek stood in the center. He held out a rod, which he had spent the past several nights carving from the branch of a fallen tree. He spun and touched each cage with the staff in turn. As he tapped each trap, a small bolt of electricity flowed out of the staff, radiated throughout the cage, and returned to the staff. After the third one, Eliska noticed the werecats no longer had a shadow, as if it had been pulled away from the werecat by the electricity. When Vivek touched the final trap, he stopped, knelt, and began chanting under his breath so softly his words could not be understood.

The surrounding shadows, stretching eastward as the sun approached the horizon, migrated toward the caged animals. When they reached the cages, the shadows detached from their objects and gathered into one huge clump. The black blob first sprouted arms and legs, a head followed. A dark creature rose and stood as tall as any mountain. It stretched out its arms and gathered up all the werecats. The physical bodies of the cats remained in the cage, but an eerie glowing mass lifted from each animal and struggled to free itself from the grasp of the monster's fists.

The massive, semi-transparent creature carried the glowing, demonic spirits far from everyone. It leaped into the air. A tremendous quake shook the ground. The land opened and the shadow and the spirits plummeted into the gaping hole.

The world around them remained shadowless. Eliska had once seen an eclipse of the sun, and the eerie feeling created by a world blanketed in shadow seemed exactly opposite to this. She felt overjoyed, and she couldn't imagine anything possibly making her sad.

After a few moments, the ground reopened and spewed forth the shadow creature. It hit the ground and splattered into fragments. The pieces scattered and returned the shadows to the mountains, trees, and all other objects...less the dead cats. They still remained shadowless. Vivek rose from his knees, raised the staff over his head, and slammed in into the ground. The stick broke, and a sickening hiss resonated as the cat shadows oozed from the broken splinters and returned to their respective bodies.

* * * *

When the few spectators quietly returned to the village, Vivek turned to Eliska. "So, do you think removing the demonic spirits was the best magic?"

"No," Eliska replied, without hesitation.

"Well, you've seen all the magic I have," Vivek explained. "I guess you'll have to find a different wizard to show you the best magic."

"No, Uncle, you did show me the best magic. It just wasn't removing the spirits."

"So you liked how I removed the boulders best after all?"

"No, that's not the best magic either."

"I'm sure neither of us thought the light show in Kingsley was the best magic; if I remember correctly, you didn't deem it magic at all."

Eliska laughed. "You're right about that."

Vivek started toward the village. Eliska could tell he was frustrated with her, as well as fatigued from the magic. It made her happy to see her uncle so humble he couldn't understand what she considered the best magic.

"Uncle," she said, running to catch him. "I'll tell you what the best magic was."

He stopped and turned to toward her.

"In Holda, we rebuilt many old structures to prepare the village for the onrush of water. Many of those levees were well past the point of needing repairs anyway, and they surely would have failed in the next few years.

"Here in Basin Hollow people were dying. We nursed them back to health. Without our help many more of them, probably even most of them, would have died. We saved their lives."

A smile played at the corner of Vivek's mouth. He shifted his gaze toward the village. Eliska knew he recognized the best magic.

"The magic you used impressed everyone, including me. But you came on this trip out of the kindness of your heart. And the best magic lies in your heart. These villagers didn't pay you for what you did. They asked for, and received, your help. But you didn't just fix their problems. You went above what they asked of you. You've enriched their lives. The personal time and care you gave to help the people… that is the best magic."

## MuseItUp
## PUBLISHING

MuseItUp Publishing
Where Muse authors entertain readers!
https://museituppublishing.com
Visit our website for more books for your reading pleasure.

You can also find us on Facebook:
http://www.facebook.com/MuseItUp
and on Twitter:
http://twitter.com/MusePublishing

CPSIA information can be obtained
at www.ICGtesting.com
Printed in the USA
FFOW02n1420011215
19129FF